The Burg

By Michelle Murray

KMP Entertainment (Publishing Division)
www.kmpentertainment.org

All characters, events and dialogue have been dramatized for

an intriguing fictional tale. Any similarity to any persons

living or dead is coincidental.

CHAPTER ONE

Devi glimpsed at the clock. It was almost six in the evening. Her former Soldier, Fletcher Faehnle, would arrive soon. She hadn't seen him in almost fifteen years. He had reached out to her on Facebook after hearing she managed various artists. He was now some sort of rapper and needed her assistance. Despite her disdain for the genre, Devi had a knack for knowing what was sellable, so she set up a meeting with him.

She no longer did artist management full time. In fact, she hardly did it at all. It was something she'd done out of necessity while she worked on her Master degree in creative writing. It paid the bills and made good use of her undergraduate degree in Entertainment Business. She had learned the hard way to be selective about whose career she guided, especially those in Hometown, America who had yet to get their feet wet in a major market.

Devi found that most hometowners had not mastered the level of professionalism needed to succeed in a major market. They weren't ready when opportunity knocked. They weren't willing to make necessary sacrifices for their futures. They refused to invest in their careers, or those of their offspring. They just wanted some magic wand to make it all happen. The worst ones were the parents who bragged relentlessly about how cute their kids were and how they should be on tv or in the movies. As soon as you told them how much an acting lesson or voice coach was, they wanted *you* to pay or they just quit altogether. Devi was over it. It was a lot of hard work for substandard pay. She much preferred writing novels and doing investigative journalism stories for a few magazines.

She was intrigued, however, when Fletcher reached out to her. She had an entire conversation with him before she realized who he was. As Devi recalled, Fletcher's Sergeant was sleeping with Fletcher's wife, Liana. Liana told Fletcher on one particular day that she was sick and wanted to sleep in, so he should just have lunch with his friends. He did, but then he stopped home to drop off chicken soup and Gatorade to her. He suspected something was amiss when he saw his Sergeant's car in the driveway. He *knew* something was amiss when he opened the front door and saw a trail of his wife's clothes and an Army uniform that led to their bedroom. When he caught them in the bedroom, he gave his Sergeant the beat down of his life.

The Sergeant, because of his wounded ego, decided to give Fletcher an Article Fifteen, demote him in rank and kick him out of the military for disrespect. Devi found out all of this through the gossip channels, and shared the version of events she had heard with her unit Commander. She was the Platoon Sergeant for the Headquarters Platoon, so she could gladly use Franklin's skillset if the Commander agreed to right this wrong. He did. Fletcher came to work for her and it was all good until he tested positive for Cocaine on a urinalysis a few weeks later.

It turned out that Fletcher had been selling the product for his former Sergeant, Sergeant First Class Habbyshaw. Even more interesting was the fact that Liana was actually Habbyshaw's girlfriend before she was Fletcher's wife. She left Habbyshaw for Fletcher, who was a regular customer of Habbyshaw's drug business. Fletcher's habit grew expensive at some point in time, so he began to sell the product for Habbyshaw. But when Fletcher caught the two in bed, he walked away from it, right after he snorted the last of the stash he had.

Devi was furious. She'd given him a chance at redemption, a chance to clear his name and start anew. Instead, he chose to do something stupid that ended his military career in shame, extra duty, and lost rank. Devi had felt no remorse for being the one who expedited his dismissal. He had shamed himself, but even worse, he had shamed her. She wanted nothing more at the time than to wash her hands of him. She hadn't given him a thought in any of the subsequent years. That is what intrigued her even more when he contacted her. He seemed to remember her with fondness.

He also seemed to have some serious talent as a musician. She'd listened briefly to three short clips he'd sent her. They seemed rather polished. So did his understanding and conversation about the steps needed to get his material to market. Devi decided to meet with him. Worst case, she'd be able to tell he was ill prepared for the Business of Entertainment and send him on his way. Best case, she'd further his career and make some money in the process. And who couldn't use extra money?

Devi looked down and noticed the stain on her shirt. It was evidence of one of her new passions: creation of floral arrangements. She loved to dry various flowers and plants, then spray paint them in a wide range of themes and colors. Today's project involved three roses, glitter and copious amounts of gold spray paint, most of which now clung to the bottom of her right sleeve.

The doorbell rang. No time to change, so she did what old NCOs do: Adapt and Overcome. She rolled her sleeves up, made an attempt to tame her curly black hair with a few pats of her hand, and strolled to the door with a smile. Before she could open it all the way, Fletcher was inside. He scooped her up in a bear hug.

"Sergeant Machesky!"

"It's good to see you, too, Faehnle," Devi noted, as she wriggled away from his grasp.

"Oh, I don't go by that anymore. Fletcher either. It's Orlando now. Orlando Beach."

"Oh, ok, Orlando. Well, come on in and have a seat on the sofa. Can I get you anything to drink? Iced tea? A water?"

"Gin and tonic if you have it."

"I don't. I have iced tea or water."

"Um, don't worry. I've got my own."

He pulled a flask out of his back pocket as he shuffled to the sofa and kicked his shoes off. He then fished a highball glass out of his jacket pocket. Devi hardly noticed, as she was distracted by his mismatched socks and the little lights on them.

"Sergeant, you want some?"

Devi paused for a moment, and examined Fletcher from head to toe. She searched for signs of the kid she once knew. They weren't there. This person was a middle aged man, with long salt and pepper hair pulled into a Samurai styled bun atop his head, and a belly which best befitted Santa Claus. His outstretched hand sported fingernails that were far too long, but beautifully manicured. His beard was also well manicured. He smelled of fruit and Jasmine.

"No, Fletcher, I'm good," Devi declared as she sat in an armchair across from him.

"Orlando. Orlando Beach."

"Yes, yes. I'm sorry. How did you come to select that name, if you don't mind me asking?"

"You remember my wife from back in the day, right?"

How could Devi forget?

"Well, I ditched her at a beach smack dab in the middle of Orlando. I had her sign the divorce papers right there. So, I love that beach. That's where I gained my freedom. It seemed only right to include that in my new persona. I couldn't remember the name of it, so I just used Orlando Beach."

Devi chewed on this for a moment. There were no beaches in the middle of Orlando. She thought to throw out names: Cocoa Beach, Vero Beach, Daytona… then she decided against it. It wouldn't change his mind. He'd still be Mr. Orlando Beach. The rationale made her chortle.

"Oh. I see. Well, that's an interesting name. You're a musician, so I don't see how it can hurt."

"Respect!" Orlando shouted with enthusiasm, as he took a long swig of whatever liquid his flask contained.

Devi wasn't sure if she should be frightened or continue to feel amused. She chose the latter before she spoke again.

"Well, I listened to the music you sent me. Do you write your own material, or just perform it? And who plays the instruments?"

"I do every single bit of it myself. I have to record it all separately and then mix and master it into one cohesive piece."

"That's impressive. Definitely not the norm. That will certainly make you more marketable."

"You sound like Gaebler. Remember him?"

"Of course I do. He was the only one who didn't lose my paperwork in that office. It got to a point that if I needed a personnel action, I'd only give him my documents."

"He used to manage me for a while. He owned a record label here, but something happened and he moved. We still keep in touch. You should give him a holler and say what's up. I'm sure he'd love to hear from you."

"Is he on social media? I'll look him up and say hi. I haven't thought about him in years. Good to hear he's doing well since the Army. Let's focus on you today, though, ok?"

"Oh, yeah. That's what's up! Just tell me what I need to do and let's get crackin'."

"Well, first, I'm going to need you to sign some paperwork allowing me to represent you. Give me your email and I will send you some paperwork to look over. I always tell people to look it over with an attorney. If you deem it a good fit, then I'll need you to sign it and return to me, along with your EPK, three mastered songs, lyric sheets and proof of ownership. After that I'll start pitching you."

"Sounds good. But I want to sign it right now. You got a printer?"

"Yes, I *have* a printer," Devi started, passively correcting his grammar. "I don't just use a generic contract, though. I personalize it to each client. I have to draw up the paperwork first and then send it to you."

"I'll wait," Orlando declared as he pulled a bag of pretzels out of his jacket pocket and offered some to Devi.

She didn't want any. She wasn't even sure she wanted to deal with this guy. Her facial expressions said as much.

"Sergeant Machesky, it is so good to see you again. I want you to know I have always had the utmost respect for you. You stuck up for me and treated me like a human being when no one else did. Even when they kicked me out of the military, you still treated me with dignity. I appreciate that. You were more than a mentor. You were a real friend when I didn't have one."

With that, Orlando began to weep. Devi was taken aback. She always taught her son that when someone considers you a friend, you need to be a friend to them. She sighed and decided to walk the walk of her own advice.

"That's kind of you to say. You were a good guy at heart. You just made some lousy choices. We are all more than the sum of our bad decisions. Hang on and let me get it typed up and then we'll get things started."

As Devi rose to get her laptop, her son entered. In many ways, he looked just like her. Same long legs. Same shoulder length curly hair. Same dimples, and same even tempered but no nonsense demeanor. Kolton, however, had an athletic physique his mother hadn't possessed since she left the Army. At six feet three inches, he was almost half a foot taller than Devi. He'd inherited an intellectual curiosity from both of his parents, as well as a love of adventure and some apparently genetic dance moves. Devi was thankful those were the only traits he had from her ex-husband.

"Is this Little Man?"

Kolton froze in his tracks. Many of Devi's friends had not seen him in years. So when they'd run into someone, it invariably meant being called "the baby," "little fellow" or some variant, and hearing stories that begin with "You don't remember me, but…" Today was no different. He had his lines down.

"Why, yes I am. Not so little anymore, though. In college. Pleasure to meet you," Kolton said with an extended hand. Orlando shook the outstretched appendage with gusto. The two instantly got lost in conversation.

Devi typed away while the two got acquainted. She had half a mind to reach out to Gaebler before she typed up the documents. She let the inclination pass and focused on preparation of Orlando's contract. When it was done, she looked it over one last time before she presented it for signature to her new client, who was now seated at her dining room table engrossed in conversation about anime with her son.

"Perfect! I love it!"

"Well, sign it and we're ready to get started."

Orlando quickly signed his name and pushed the paperwork back to Devi.

"Finally. Someone who understands my genius, my gift."

Devi just smiled uncomfortably, unsure of what to say. Kolton's eyes narrowed. He'd spent half an hour or so in conversation with Orlando. The guy was no genius, not by any stretch of the imagination.

"People usually persecute me. Especially when they find out my secret," Orlando continued.

"Your secret?" Devi queried curiously, unsure of what could be more spectacular than the *why* of him getting out of the military.

Orlando leaned in. Devi leaned out. Kolton, an innate people watcher, pressed his lips together to stifle his laughter. He put a little distance between himself and Orlando before he pulled his head back and pressed his shoulders forward. Devi wasn't big on secrets and Drama Kings, so Kolton suspected that whatever flowed next from Orlando's mouth just might get him tossed out of the house.

"Yes, my secret. I don't tell people this. Only my girlfriend knows. But if you and I are going to work together, I have to come clean."

"Ok…" Devi uttered with a hint of curiosity.

"I'm Jesus, and people just don't get it. They think it's a sin for me to be rapping if I'm Jesus. But my father says it's all good. I need to do me. Ya feel me?"

Kolton tilted his head away and chuckled silently. Devi pushed lightly on her diaphragm in an effort to contain her own laughter. She began to fidget with the paperwork on the table.

"Oh, you're Jesus. That must be rough, having to keep such a secret."

"It is! But I am so thankful God led me to you. Now I can be my true creative self and make things happen for us both."

Devi began to rub her forehead. Her eyes were closed. Kolton knew this was not a good sign, not for Orlando, anyway. Devi internally weighed the pros and cons of working with Orlando. He seemed a little crazy. Not psychotic or dangerous, like he'd kill you or steal your purse, but definitely off his rocker. She wrinkled her nose for a brief moment. Kolton's heart pounded. He was ready to spring into action if Devi needed help to usher Orlando out the front door. Then Devi's muscles relaxed and she smiled.

"Ok. Well, you'd better get out of here and get me the things I need if you want to get started. My email is on your copy of the contract. Send it there for me to look over."

Orlando hugged Devi, then hurried out the door. Kolton's mouth opened, but nothing came out. He ran his fingers through his hair and put a fist to his lips.

"You aren't seriously going to work with him, are you?"

"I don't know."

"You don't know?"

"I don't know. I'm going to get in touch with Gaebler to find out what Fletcher's deal is before I decide."

"Orlando."

"Yeah, yeah. Or Jesus, or whomever else he wants to be. A lot of musicians are eccentric. If he can comply with how things work in this business, I'll work with him for bit and get him started. Then I'll push him off on some other unsuspecting soul."

"What? No. Terrible idea. Don't work with him."

"Well, we have a partially signed contract now. If I do some digging and see that he's not as bad as he appears, I'll sign it and work with him. The first whiff of trouble, though, and I'm done."

"What! Why even give him a chance?"

"I can't explain. I guess it's because he's a former Soldier. We went to combat together. There's a bond. You wouldn't understand."

Kolton stared blankly. Devi was correct. He didn't understand. He trusted her judgement, though, so he'd leave it alone. For now. His eyebrows squeezed slightly together before he spoke.

"All right. Sounds like a plan. I have a video game to play. Let me know what you find out."

Devi blew him a kiss as he bounded up the stairs to his bedroom. One thing was certain. Kolton always had her back when no one else did. On top of that, he was a great kid, a joy to be around. He was focused and goal oriented, too. He'd finished high school at fifteen and a half, and would earn his Bachelor degree in a little more of than a year, just shy of his eighteenth birthday. Devi felt blessed to call him son. She smiled as she went back to her desk and opened her laptop.

She paused for a moment as she tried to remember Gaebler's first name. Was it Shawn? Steven? Shane? She tried all three on Facebook and hit the jackpot with Shane. She sent him a message.

> *Hi, there! I don't know if you remember me, but we earned our combat patches on the same deployment when we were both stationed at Fort Bliss. I was talking to Fletcher Faehnle today, and he brought you up. I hear you've found much success since the Army! Good for you! I always love to hear about former Battle Buddies doing well. I have a few questions about Fletcher Maybe you could provide some answers. He's trying to break into the music scene. He says you used to represent him. Well, he's asked me to represent him now. So, as I said above, I have some questions before he and I move forward. I hope to hear back from you soon.*

Devi reviewed the message three times before she sent it. Sending messages to people she didn't know well always unnerved her a little bit. Was her tone ok? Did she have any spelling errors? Was she being too forward? Her head began to swim. She pushed 'send' before her thoughts got the best of her.

She scanned the message one more time. She wanted to make sure she hadn't missed an error. As she was reading the last sentence, she got a reply.

Hello. Of course I remember you. Most beautiful Sergeant I ever saw lol. How are you doing? How's the other Sergeant Machesky! I hope he is doing well, too. And your son? How is he? As for Faehnle, he's ummmmmmmmm special. I thought he had changed his name to Florida orange juice or something?

Devi burst into laughter at the Florida orange juice comment. She frowned at the question about her ex-husband, though. She couldn't be too offended over it. Gaebler would definitely have no way of knowing she had divorced that lying, cheating chump ten years prior.

Glad you remember me. We are well on my end. I've been divorced about ten years now. I retired a few years ago from the

Army. I went back to school and got a second Bachelor degree in Entertainment Business and a Master degree in Creative Writing, with an emphasis in screenwriting. I've written a couple of novels and produced some of my own filmed content. Hoping to get a full time gig with one of the studios in LA. I'm still in El Paso full time, but I go back and forth to LA when I have work. I get gigs through an agency right now so I can build my resume. My son and I actually started a little production company together. When I was in school I did artist management to pay the bills. When I graduated, I passed most of my roster to some other agencies. Anyway, Faehnle reached out to me through Facebook to represent him. Gotta love Facebook! I have a few questions about his, um, mental competence. How was he to work with? Did you have any issues with him I should know about? Like I said, it's not really something I do much anymore, but he really needs the help. Would you take him back as a client? If he is mentor-able, I'll do it. If not, Bye Felicia! Lol

Shane laughed out loud at the message and quickly responded.

I don't do music anymore but if I did I would probably take him back. Did he do something that made you think you need to proceed with caution?

Devi quickly responded:

Other than telling me he believes he is Jesus, not really.

Shane read the reply twice to make sure he wasn't imagining things.

Jesus, huh? Oh, boy!

Devi contemplated before she sent her next message:

So, do I take him on as a client or not?

Shane wasn't sure what to say. He had never had problems, but that's because he knew Faehnle on a level he was pretty sure Sergeant Machesky did not. He replied:

He's harmless, but be careful. Here's my number if you ever need anything else. 541.555.1292

Devi felt a wave of relief at the nod to proceed with Faehnle.

Sounds good. Thanks. Where is a 541 area code?

Shane typed:

Oregon. Ever been here?

Devi:

No, but it's ironic you are there. My son and I are thinking of touring one of our shows and I had plans to drive up there and look at venues around Portland. Are you close to there?

Shane:

No. I'm a few hours south. I'm about a hundred and twenty five miles north of the Oregon California border.

Devi:

Oh, ok. If I get up that way to look at venues, I'll give you a call. Maybe we can do lunch or something. It's always nice to catch up with old friends.

Shane:

Yes. Do that. It's really pretty here. We have several venues I bet you'd like.

Devi:

What city are you in?

Shane:

Roseburg.

Devi:

Never heard of it. Googling it now.

She paused the conversation to peruse online photos of the town. It was one of the most picturesque places she had ever seen. It was much prettier than the photos she had seen of Portland.

Wow! I just looked it up. Very beautiful. Are you from there?

Shane:

Yep. Born and raised. If you ever want to come up, let me know. I have plenty of room and you and your son are welcome to stay here.

Devi:

Awww. Thanks. That's kind. I'll keep you posted. I was thinking of making a trip in a few months. If it pans out, I'll definitely link up.

Shane:

Cool.

Devi:

Ok. I'm not going to talk your ear off all night. I'll let you go. Thanks for the info. Take care.

Shane:

If it's all right with you, I'm going to send you a friend request.

Devi:

Sure! Don't be a stranger. I'll text my cell number to your phone.

Shane:

Deal. Have a good evening.

Devi:

You, too.

The Facebook friend request came before she closed out her messages. She accepted right away. Devi studied his profile picture. She remembered him being handsome in their Army days. He'd aged well. Same handsome features and beautiful headful of wavy hair. It was completely grey now, but was gorgeous nonetheless. She saw no evidence of a wife or girlfriend. She vaguely remembered him being in the middle of a divorce when she last worked with him. It made her a little sad that he was alone. He was always such a nice guy.

She also remembered having a crush on him when they worked together. She'd invited him to join her platoon at her house for dinner one Sunday, right before her divorce was official. She was reassigned to another unit shortly thereafter and that was that. She was too busy fielding a new design of the PATRIOT Missile system in the years that followed to give him further thought. She had wondered what became of him more than a few times over the years. It was nice to reconnect. She hoped he felt the same.

Seventeen hundred miles away, Shane perused Devi's Facebook. She was more beautiful than he recalled. He was always attracted to her. Two things always kept his courage to approach her suppressed: the fact that she outranked him by multiple paygrades, coupled with the fact that her husband, who also outranked him by a few paygrades, worked in the same Battalion. He was glad to know neither thing was an issue anymore. He still found her wildly attractive. He wanted to get to know her better. He hoped she felt the same.

CHAPTER TWO

Seventeen months had passed since the first encounter between Devi and Shane. They called each other first thing each morning. They text all through the day, and then stayed on the phone again for hours each night. It was as if they had become teenagers all over again.

Shane had disclosed to Devi that he was an animal lover like her, and he shared many of her interests: photography, horses, SCUBA diving, golf, camping and, despite his long hours as an administrator at the VA hospital, he regularly volunteered in the community. Devi loved the fact that he volunteered regularly at his church like she did. She worked with the high school kids and young adults ministries. She also was a door greeter, who sincerely welcomed each parishioner with a hearty smile each time she was there. Her son volunteered at church, too. Devi felt her most important duty in life was to help her son carve out a relationship with God, so she took this task quite seriously. She was pleased to know that Shane took it just as seriously. Both he and his son, he had shared, had very close relationships with God. And volunteered together at church, as well

Devi reflected upon this as she sipped her morning glass of Perrier. Some people drank coffee. She drank sparkling water. Her phone rang. It was Shane.

"Good morning, Beautiful."

"Good morning to you, too, my sweet friend. It's nice to hear your voice."

"You know, you're kind of like my girlfriend without really being my girlfriend."

"What?" Devi laughed.

"Seriously. Think about how much time we spend talking to each other. We tell each other everything. When we're happy, we want to talk to each other. When we are angry, we want to talk to each other. When we are doing something fun, we tell each other. So like I said, you're like my girlfriend."

"I guess you're right," Devi giggled.

"So, are we doing this or what?"

Devi grew quiet. Her divorce was finalized ten years and nine months earlier. She had only dated one man, quite briefly. He "forgot" to mention he had a wife and six kids. After that, she never gave another man her attention. Shane was different. She really enjoyed him, and he didn't have a wife and six kids. She'd made sure of that when they first connected. He was a very single dad, with one son the same age as her own. She liked the fact that he was not only involved in his son's life, but that he raised him alone after his mom decided illegal drugs were far more important than being a mother. Devi asked herself would she want to go back to a life without Shane's company. The answer was no.

"I'm in if you're in," she told him.

Shane smiled from ear to ear. He couldn't contain his excitement. He let out a soul-stirring whoop of delight.

"Are you ok over there?"

"I'm perfect. Perrrrr-fect. I'm glad you said yes. Now I can make it Facebook official."

"What are we? Twelve?"

"No. I'm just so happy. I want the entire world to know we are a *we*! Don't you?"

"Sure I do. But give me a minute to talk to my kid. He barely even knows you exist."

"Oh, he knows I exist. I sent him a Facebook friend request last night."

"That's interesting. He didn't mention it. Well, I've told him about you, and he can see how much time we spend on the phone. But I'd rather tell him about this *we* thing before he sees it on Facebook."

"Too late. I already put it on there."

"What? When?"

"Just now. Don't worry. He won't see it before you talk to him."

Kolton barreled down the steps and into the kitchen right at that moment. He made a beeline for his mother. He could see she was on the phone, so he held up his phone, pointed to something on the screen, and mouthed "What is this?" Devi looked. Kolton had Shane's Facebook page pulled up. He pointed to the relationship status that had her name listed.

"Shane, let me call you back."

"Ok. Have a good day. I can't wait to talk to you again soon!"

"Same."

Devi disconnected the call, then stared at Kolton's phone screen like a toddler caught with her hand in the cookie jar before dinner.

"It's not at all what it looks like."

Kolton was amused. His mother always told him the truth. Always. She was as dependable as London's trusty Old Ben. He didn't believe her a bit at the moment, though.

"Yeah? What is it then?"

"I told him not to do that. I, well, I…"

"Who *is* this guy?"

"I told you. He is a very old friend. I've known him for more than twenty years."

"Why haven't I heard of him then?"

Devi gave Kolton a blank stare. It was clear that though the wheels spun in her brain, they stopped on no definitive answer.

"You just haven't. I don't know. He was in the Army with me. We went to combat together. I know him. He's a good guy."

"But why don't I know him then? You've never even spoken of him. I know all your other Army friends. Heck, I even know some of the Soldiers you didn't like."

"Look. I changed units. He got out of the Army. We lost touch. Now we are back in touch. The whole relationship thing on Facebook was like a joke. He was joking saying I'm like his girlfriend without really being his girlfriend, and I didn't even know he put that on there. I swear."

Kolton studied Devi momentarily. She was telling the truth.

"But you like him."

"I don't dislike him. I don't know. It's hard to explain."

Kolton pulled out a chair next to Devi and had a seat. He took a sip from her glass. He gagged and made a face. He was not a sparkling water kind of guy.

"The way I feel about this water is the way I feel about this guy. Who *is* he?"

'Funny you should ask. You know how we were talking about touring one of our shows on the west coast? Well, he lives in Oregon and says there are some pretty cool venues up there that we might be interested in. I told him we'd take a trip up to check things out. Then you can meet each other. Well, you can meet him. He has seen you plenty of times."

"As a baby doesn't count."

"…and he has a son your age. The two of you can hang out or whatever guys your age do."

"Fine. Whatever floats your boat. When were you thinking of going up there?"

"Your birthday is in a couple of weeks on the twentieth, and I want us to be here in town for that so you can celebrate with your friends. I was thinking we could leave the next day, take our time driving, and try to be there by Friday. The twenty third."

"Do we even have clothes for there? Doesn't it snow? It barely hits sixty degrees here in winter. I know we don't have clothes for that."

Devi had considered this. In winter, she typically threw on a sweater and hoped for the best. She hadn't owned a real winter coat since she lived in Germany nearly twenty years prior.

"We have to drive through Los Angeles. We'll pick something up over there, or a little further north. Before we hit Oregon."

In the blink of an eye, road trip day was upon them. As always, Devi had the car loaded down. She always said "It's better to have it and not need it than need it and not have it." She'd actually proven this to be true on a number of occasions, so Kolton no longer complained or made jokes.

By the time they made it from their home in El Paso to Los Angeles, it was almost dinner time, and nearly seventy degrees. They searched two malls and several boutiques, but found no suitable winter clothing.

"It's still bikini weather, so the only winter clothing I can offer you is a Laker's hoodie. Sorry," one clerk teased.

They decided to wait until they got to Oregon to find winter clothing. By the time they got to Sacramento, Devi wondered if this was a mistake. The temperature dipped by twenty degrees. But it was late and no stores were open. Kolton assured her they'd be fine until they hit Oregon. They both had sweaters with them to keep them warm until then, he pointed out.

It was nearly 2 AM as they approached Mt. Shasta. A sign blinked that said "Snow Chains required." There didn't seem to be *that* much snow, but the digital warning made Devi nervous. She didn't have snow chains. For that matter, she didn't really even know what they were, or how to use them if she did possess them.

The night was far darker than Devi was used to. She was accustomed to street lights and luminescence from the city. Here, it was just her, the mountain, and a moon whose light was stifled by fir trees and snow flurries. The wind blasted the car, which frightened Devi a bit. The heavy fog made Devi wish she had not agreed to this trip.

Kolton was asleep. She was glad. That meant she didn't have to hide her fear. She could squint and furrow her brow without her son asking what was wrong. More so, she didn't have to lie in reply.

Devi instinctively turned on her radio. That was something she always did in poor weather conditions. Static. Lots of static. She flipped through channels and finally got something on an AM weather station. They were calling the storm system a bomb cyclone.

"That sounds scary," she whispered aloud.

The broadcaster said the storm system had moved into northern California and Southern Oregon, and packed quite a punch. The blowing snow and dense fog confirmed this. Devi cut the radio off. She didn't want to hear any more.

She guessed she was approximately sixty or seventy miles from the Oregon border. Then she had only a hundred and twenty five more to go after that. This deterred her from her desire to turn the car around and head home to Texas.

She stopped for gas in a town called Weed. It was still pitch black, but the gas station's lights were like a beacon of hope. Devi slowly pulled up to the pump and took in her surroundings as she turned the car off. There was a grocery store, Taco Bell, Starbucks and Burger King. They were all closed. She was a hungry, but it seemed like a peanut butter sandwich and bottled water would have to do. She gobbled down a sandwich almost as fast as she could fix it.

She decided she'd get gas before she woke up Kolton. She fished her debit card out of her wallet and stepped out of the car to swipe it at the pump. The thermal underwear and three layers of sweaters she wore were no match for the bone chilling cold. She'd forgotten to change shoes in Sacramento, so she wore only flip flops. The thought of heading home crossed her mind once again. She let it pass.

That's when she noticed there was no place to swipe her card. She'd have to go in to pay. She turned toward the entrance of the store. It had to be fifty feet away. That was much too far, she thought. She decided to wake Kolton up and have him go instead.

A yowl escaped his lips as he exited the car. Though he had been born when Devi and her ex-husband were stationed in Germany, he had spent the majority of his life in the desert of West Texas, with frequent travel to Southern California and Southern Florida. He was definitely a creature of the sun. He sprinted into the store.

In a few moments, the pump came to life. Devi quickly pumped the gas and jumped back in the car. Kolton wrapped himself into a cocoon with a blanket that had been on the back seat. The expression on his mostly hidden face said "I told you this wasn't a good idea. I'm grumpy about it. But I'm your ride or die, so let's do this."

"We're almost there," Devi proclaimed as she started the car.

"It's twenty six degrees with zero visibility according to the cashier in the store. She said we should probably stay put til daybreak."

"We're almost there. I think we've endured the worst."

"The store clerk doesn't think so, but ok. Let's go ahead and get there so we can get back home."

Devi chuckled to herself and pulled out of the gas station. As they neared the Oregon border fifty three miles later, Devi couldn't see at all. This alarmed her. She had never driven in such conditions. She reflected back to when she lived in Germany. The Germans were smart. They closed the roads in such conditions and people obeyed the directive to stay home.

She slowed to less than ten miles per hour. It didn't help. In addition to the snow that fell, a thicker fog rolled in, as well. Devi slowed down even more. She was inches from the bumper of a semi-truck she had not seen before. The truck pulled off to the side of the road. Devi decided to follow. One thing she knew for sure: when a trucker was cautious, a car should be twice as cautious.

She looked at her watch. The sun would be up soon, and she was tired. Though her car idled, ice formed on the windshield. She took in the treacherous conditions that surrounded her. She didn't see any spin-outs or accidents. Maybe the truckers were just weary and wanted a quick nap. Devi decided to take her chances and press forward to her destination. She pulled back onto the roadway slowly.

After about thirty miles, the snow had disappeared. The road in front of her was clear. She was relieved. She saw a sign that said Roseburg was 85 miles more. A smile crawled across her lips. Like a youngster who anticipated goodies from Santa on Christmas, Devi was excited to see Shane face to face.

She had driven the last eight hours or so with rollers in her hair. She glanced over at the floorboard beneath Kolton's feet to make sure her make up bag was still there. It was. Her eyes darted to her rearview mirror. She tilted it a hair so she could see herself. Hottest mess she had ever seen. She decided to pull off at the next exit to spruce up a bit.

Unlike Texas, or even California, there were no signs of an all-night gas station or truck stop every few exits. The foreboding trees sent a chill up Devi's spine, but she pulled off the freeway anyway. There was no streetlight, so Devi used her SCUBA flashlight. She smiled as she did. Kolton made fun of her for keeping it in the car. She always told him it would be handy in an emergency. And it was.

Kolton snored softly as Devi did her make up. She removed the rollers from her hair and ran her fingers through it. She approved of the person who stared at her in the mirror. She decided to text Shane and let him know she'd be there soon.

"*Yipee!*" came his reply.

Devi chuckled, but had to admit, she, too, wanted to say Yipee! She was extremely excited to finally see Shane in person. They'd missed the last twenty years together. She didn't want to waste another minute more. She tossed her flashlight onto the back seat and began her journey again.

In just over an hour, she neared her exit. She was currently at exit one twenty. She would meet Shane at exit one twenty five. She pulled her phone out and called Shane to let him know.

"Hey! I'm almost there. I'm five exits away."

"Yay! I'm already here waiting on you. Just exit at one twenty-five, then go to the right. There is a Smoke Shop right there. You'll see me in the parking lot. Burgundy Jeep."

"Got it. See you soon."

She disconnected the call, and felt the anticipation increase within her. She looked over at Kolton. He wasn't asleep. He eyed her suspiciously.

"Who *is* this guy?"

"I told you. An old friend."

"If you say so," Kolton teased.

"Oh! Here's our exit!"

Devi followed the winding exit to Garden Valley Street. It was dark, but she could see the lone car off to her right. Shane was exactly where he said he'd be, in the parking lot of a place apparently called The Smoke Shop. The simple name made Devi smile to herself. Shane rolled his window down at that moment, and her smile grew in volume. He knew it was for him. Devi seemed to telepathically agree.

"Well, hi there, Beautiful."

Kolton resisted the urge to throw up.

"Hey, Handsome. Thanks for meeting us here. I knew it was going to be dark and I'd probably get lost."

"No problem. Come on. Follow me."

Shane took off like a greyhound on a race track. Devi reflected to something she always said. "When someone is following you, drive like they are and make sure they don't get lost." Drivers who didn't do so irked her. She let the thought pass, and drove a tad more aggressively so she could keep up.

Down the street, up the hill, down the hill, up another hill, around a winding road and finally, they were at Shane's house. He whipped into the driveway and had the garage door up and waiting on Devi before she could get out of her car. She rolled her window down to chide him for driving so fast, but he spoke first.

"You can park in there. I'll park in the driveway."

Devi was thankful and gratefully pulled in.

"I've never seen a one car garage before. Interesting."

"Really? That's how most of them are up here."

A gust of brisk January air hit Devi through her open window. She still wore flip flops and inadequate clothing.

"Come on in and get warm," Shane beckoned.

Devi turned to Kolton and tossed him her keys.

"Park it and meet me inside. I'm sure his son is anxious to meet you."

Kolton looked non-plussed but eagerly took the keys. His mother rarely allowed him to drive with her in the vehicle, something about one of her Soldiers and a roll-over. At any rate, he always chomped at the bit to drive, even if only for a moment. Before he could switch over to the driver side seat, Devi and Shane were already in the house.

"I'm glad you're here. It's really nice to see you," Shane said as he reached for Devi's hand.

She clasped her fingers with his and smiled. Before she could say anything, he kissed her. She felt like she was going to melt. As if on cue, Shane scooped her up and carried her down the hall to his bedroom. He kicked the door closed behind him and placed Devi on the bed. He sat next to her and smiled. They embraced tightly. Devi pulled back to look at him.

"What is it?"

"Nothing. You're just far more handsome than I recalled."

She lightly caressed his face. Shane smiled, then pulled her close once more. The scent of her hair filled him with desire. He ran his fingers through her Devi's mane, as he pulled her closer and kissed her forehead.

"Hey! Where are you guys?" Kolton called from the front foyer.

Shane and Devi giggled like school-children. Kolton's size thirteen footsteps approached them. Shane stole one more kiss just before the knock came at the door.

"Come on in!" Shane bellowed.

Kolton came in slowly. Suspiciously. He eyed his mother, then took in the surroundings. He settled his gaze on Shane. He didn't know what was going on, but he didn't like it. There was something about this guy he didn't think he'd ever like. He directed his attention toward Devi.

"Did you want me to get the bags out of the car?"

"Yes. Absolutely. We both need a shower and our bed clothes."

"Are you going to help me?"

It was more of a suggestion than a question. Devi was amused. Was Kolton being protective?

"Yes, here I come."

Devi got up, but stopped and turned to Shane, who still sat on the bed.

"Is your son asleep? I just realized I didn't tell him hi!"

"My son?"

Shane looked confused.

"Yes, your son. Paul? Don't you think it's rude for me not to greet him?" Devi jokingly pointed out.

"He's not here."

Kolton's eyes widened in astonishment. The sun was about to come up. His mother would never let him stay out that late. Devi look intrigued.

"Oh, ok. I guess I'll meet him when he gets home."

"He's not living here. His grandparents got real sick recently so he went to go help them out for a while. Down in California. He'll be back in a few weeks, though. He actually just left earlier today. Thought I told you."

Devi shook her head. He had not. They had been so consumed in her plans to visit, it had probably just slipped his mind. She had looked forward to Kolton having another young person to hang out with. She knew he wasn't too keen on the trip in the first place. She knew Paul had some of the same interests, so she had hoped they'd have plenty to talk about and the trip wouldn't be a total wash for Kolton.

"Well, where do I put my stuff when I get it out of the car?" asked a weary Kolton.

"In Paul's room. Come on. I'll show you."

Devi watched the two as they left. She was thrilled to finally have them both in the same room at once. She knew Kolton would eventually warm up to Shane. He was just so used to it only being the two of them for so long, Devi knew it was a task of sorts to ask him to take someone else into their fold, but she had faith that he would.

Later, when Devi had showered, she cuddled next to Shane on the couch. They stared into each other's eyes often. Each was ecstatic to have the other near. Both were full of pure adoration and warmth for the other. An old black and white movie was on, and they held hands as they watched.

They fell asleep holding hands, snuggled next to each other on the sofa.

The next few days were a whirlwind of hand-holds, sights seen, jokes told, board games played and good old fashioned getting to know each other. On the way home, Kolton admitted that even though he was still a little cautious, he had enjoyed himself. Devi was elated to hear this.

"I only thought one thing was kind of strange."

"Oh, really? And what was that?" Devi asked.

"He didn't have any photos up of his son. None. Not a single one. Didn't you say he's a photographer, too? That makes it extra weird."

Devi chewed on this for a moment. She had thought it a wee bit odd, but she let the thought pass. He was a guy, after all. Some guys just weren't in to photos. She shared this with Kolton.

"Yeah, but he had pictures up of himself. All over the place."

"Well, if that's the only fault you kind find with him, I'd say that's pretty good."

"It's not really the only thing. I also thought it was weird he said I stayed in his son's room, but none of his son's stuff was in there."

"What do you mean?"

"I mean none of his things were in the room. No clothes. No video games. No shoes. No anything. Also, it was a futon, not an actual bed, so I don't really think that's anybody's room."

Devi also thought this was odd, but she didn't say so.

"Well, he did say Paul had just gone to stay a few weeks with his grandparents."

"Who takes all of their things for a few weeks?"

No one Devi knew, but apparently Paul did.

"Maybe he just wanted to feel at home while he is at his grandparents' home?"

Kolton gave Devi a side-eye, then chuckled.

"It doesn't even matter. We're on our way home," Kolton said as he gave a two fingered command for his mom to whisk him away more quickly and not get lost in the details of the visit with Shane.

Devi smiled, switched lanes and passed the truck in front of her. The snow she'd encountered on the way up had begun to melt away, and she had fairly clear roads as she left Oregon in her rear-view mirror. She already missed Shane and couldn't wait until he came to visit her in a month for her birthday. She daydreamed about him, to Kolton's chagrin, the entire way home.

A year of back and forth visits happened before Shane asked Devi to marry him and move to Oregon. He had two years left until retirement, he'd shared, and she had flexibility as a writer to do her job from anywhere, so it just made better sense for Devi to come to Oregon until he retired and then he'd come to Texas. Devi agreed to both counts. She disliked the miles between them, as did he. They set a date that was still nearly two years out, but Devi wanted to have ample time to plan such an affair.

Kolton was not pleased, not at all. Something about Shane still didn't set right with him, but he simply could not pinpoint what it was. He told his mother as much.

"Can you please just give him a chance? He's not as bad as you think. Hasn't he been nice to you?"

"Yeah, I guess. Look, I'm just here so that when things fall apart between you and your little boyfriend I can help you get your stuff and move back home. Whatever floats your boat. Let's do this."

Devi considered that Kolton's way of giving his blessing. She decided to quit while she was ahead and say no more on the subject. She got a box, and they started to pack. She wasn't taking everything. Just a few essentials to make it feel like home until she got back to Texas. Everything else would go in storage. Cheers to new beginnings, she thought to herself as she wrapped her vase.

CHAPTER THREE

The first order of business for Devi was to explore the town and transition from visitor to local. She found the luncheon schedule for the local Rotary club, and joined them her second day in town. She'd been a Rotarian her entire adult life, so she knew she could find a club in just about every locale in the world.

She linked up with the Boy Scouts, as she had been a leader from the time her son was a Cub Scout until he earned his Eagle Scout rank. She learned where the best produce was sold, which store had the best meat, which stores had the best prices, where the bookstore was, and where the locals liked to hang out. Then she began to read up on the town's history and search for any stories that needed to be told to the rest of the world. She hadn't quit her job as an investigative journalist for Origin Tales Magazine, and she had a deadline to meet. She agreed to still submit stories about things that shaped America.

She soon found one that they wanted written up and submitted within the next ten days.

Several people, including Shane, had told Devi about The Roseburg blast of 1959. Devi had never heard about it, but it had apparently changed and shaped the way explosives were transported and handled around the entire country. On August 7, 1959, a fire broke out at Dent Gerretsen Building Supply Company. A truck that carried more than thirteen-thousand pounds of explosives had been parked on the adjacent street. The fire at Gerretsen, as the company was known, ignited the dynamite and ammonium nitrate load and leveled an eight city block radius. A huge crater was left behind at the explosion site. It was fifty two feet in diameter and approximately twelve feet deep, up to twenty feet deep in some places.

Damage resulted for more than thirty blocks. Windows were broken as far as seven miles away. People reported hearing the blast nearly seventy miles away in the city of Eugene. More than three hundred businesses were damaged. Seventy two were deemed structurally unsafe and had to have major repairs. Another twelve buildings were condemned. Fourteen people died in the blast, and a hundred-twenty or so others were injured.

As a result of the blast, stricter explosives transport laws for both public and private carriers came into existence. The Interstate Commerce Commission oversaw their enforcement. New laws came about regarding explosive marking and signage. The ICC also enforced these regulations and laws. Another thing the blast did was cause towns across America to prepare disaster response plans. Roseburg had no such plan in place at the time of the blast. The chaos and devastation that followed the blast made it sorely evident that not having one had been a huge mistake.

From what Devi could tell, the trucker who had transported the explosives, George Rutherford, had parked the truck adjacent to Gerretsen because the company had a security guard on duty. His employer, Pacific Powder, had been fearful of night time thievery, and forbade him to park the truck at the explosive storage depot outside of town when he slept for the night at the Umpqua Hotel, as was the usual, and safest, protocol.

Rutherford had been awakened by all the commotion of the fire. He hurried downstairs from his hotel room to go move his truck. Before he could reach his destination, the truck exploded and knocked him unconscious. Though he survived, he carried much survivor's guilt with him for the rest of his life. Devi wished he'd been alive for her to interview. Perhaps he still had living family members who could give commentary from his point of view. She'd find out tomorrow. Right now, she wanted to get Orlando Beach's electronic press kit submitted to some buyers.

"Kolton, come here," she called downstairs to his bedroom.

"I'll be right there!" was the reply.

Devi looked at the papers sprawled out on her desk. Most of them had to do with PR for Orlando Beach. He'd wanted to take his time and produce "perfect" content for

Devi to shop around for him, so this was the first time she'd had everything together to pitch for him.

"Hey, give this a listen. It's Orlando Beach's music, finally. I've got a few labels in mind for it, but I want to hear your thoughts," Devi said to Kolton as he approached her desk.

"Oh, 'Jesus' finally sent you some music?"

"Yeah…" Devi laughed.

Devi clicked play on the first track. Ten seconds in, Kolton held his hand up in a "stop" motion. Devi pressed pause. She gave Kolton a quizzical look.

"That's not his music. That is a Michael Jackson song."

"People do covers all the time, Kolton."

"No. Like that IS Michael Jackson. That's not even the Jesus dude."

Devi sat up a little straighter and hit play again. Sure enough. It was absolutely Michael Jackson. She chuckled and hit stop. What did she expect from a guy who called himself Orlando Beach?

"Ok. Well, that was fun while it lasted. I found a story I want to check out. Pretty interesting. I guess they had some kind of explosion or something here and that's why we have laws for transporting explosives now. It happened back in the fifties, but I'm going to see if I can find some survivors tomorrow. Want to come with me?"

"Where?"

"Old timers always hang out at the VA. Thought I'd ask around over there first."

"No thanks. You guys spend hours talking about disability ratings and war stories. I know yours verbatim. I'm good," Kolton teased before he ran off downstairs again.

Devi leaned back in her chair and noticed the trash can was overflowing. She was about to call for Kolton again but decided to just take it out herself. She laughed aloud about Orlando Beach's supposedly perfect music as she pulled the bag out of the trash can and walked outside.

She took in the scenery around her as she deposited the trash in the can outside. It was beautiful. Douglas fir trees, flowers and plenty of green everywhere you looked. She had her eyes fixed on the mountain. It was beautiful. She didn't even hear Shane when he pulled into the driveway.

"Hey, good looking!" he smiled. Then his face turned serious.

"What's wrong?"

"Who's that? Why is she staring at you like that?"

Devi whirled around. She didn't see anyone.

"Who?" she asked.

Shane leaned his head out of his opened window. He craned his neck around Devi. He didn't see the woman anymore either.

"Nobody. I guess I'm tired. That tree looked like a woman."

"Come on in and let's eat dinner. Tell me about your day."

Unbeknownst to Devi, a pair of eyes was fixated on her as she entered the house.

CHAPTER FOUR

The next morning, Devi's eyes blinked open after several minutes. She squinted to see the time on her cell phone. It was five minutes til six. She popped out of bed and darted into the kitchen. Shane took his last swig of coffee and grabbed his keys.

"You didn't wake me up," Devi whispered as she gave him a good morning hug.

"You looked so tired. I just thought I'd let you rest for once. But I have to admit. I did miss that fabulous breakfast you usually make me," Shane said with a smile.

"I can make you something quick."

"No, it's ok. I have to run. I have a meeting as soon as I walk in the door this morning."

Devi nodded that she understood. She sauntered over to the counter and grabbed a blueberry muffin. They were day old, but still pretty tasty. It was better than nothing. As an Associate Director of the VA Hospital, he had to be in awfully early and usually stayed a tad bit later than everyone else, too. Devi thought the least she could do was make sure he started his day with something in his belly.

Shane grabbed the muffin and kissed her on her cheek.

"Thanks! I might not make it home for lunch, but I should be home early."

Then out the door he went. Before Devi could even move, there was a knock at the door. Shane must have forgotten his key. She ran to open the door for him. Much to her surprise, it wasn't Shane. It was Wanda.

"Wanda? Is that you?"

"Yes, girl. You going to leave me standing out here on this porch or what?"

Devi motioned for her to come in and then gave her a tight hug.

"What on earth are you doing here? In this tiny town of all the places on earth…" Devi questioned, shocked.

"I should be asking *you* that. My people are from up this way. A little town up the road actually. There's more work here in Roseburg. I live right there, across the street."

"What! Well, I'll be. Talk about a small world. Well, I guess you could say a man brought me here."

The two woman broke into a raucous laughter. Devi waved Wanda over to the sofa. She glanced at the coffee pot that was calling out to her from the kitchen. She started to pour two cups. She decided against it and instead grabbed the whole coffee pot and two cups and brought it into the living room. She remembered how much Wanda liked coffee. Devi wasn't really a coffee drinker, but she wanted to social.

"I haven't seen you in so long. I can't believe it's been almost, what, two years now since I saw you. I was in the middle of retiring and starting a business when everything happened. I'm sorry I didn't stay in better contact. How has life been treating you since Uncle Clem died?"

Wanda bowed her head. Tears formed in the corner of her eyes. She tried to swallow, but a million emotions seemed to be stuck in her throat, and made it hard. She closed her eyes for a moment and then made eye contact with Devi, who was now seated beside her.

"That's actually what I wanted to talk to you about."

Devi now regretted opening that can of worms. Wanda and Clem both had drinking and drugging issues. As such, they always ran low on money and asked any and everybody for "a couple dollars" til payday. Clem had died of an accidental overdose, or so Devi had heard, and she honestly thought Wanda would have been right behind him. Their daughter Allison had the same issues. Devi loved them, but she kept a good distance. Her wallet couldn't take too many interactions with them. Devi drew Wanda in for another hug, then braced for the ask.

"It's Allison. She's gone, too."

Devi sat up straight and paused before she said "What do you mean she's gone, too?"

"She's gone. She's dead. They stole her from me."

"Who stole her from you?" Devi said as she stood up, awash with emotion.

"That's why I came over here. I heard you become some kind of investigator or something after you got out of the service, right?"

"No. I'm a writer."

"But you investigate stuff, right?"

"Let's talk about Allison. *Who* took her from you? You mean someone killed her?"

"The police did it."

"What happened? Like at a traffic stop or something? Or was she committing a crime? Was she selling dope again?"

"None of that. But they drugged my daughter up and left her for dead and that motel down the freeway and said she overdosed. She didn't overdose."

Devi looked at Wanda, who was clearly in denial. Allison was absolutely a junkie, so she probably did overdose. Like father like daughter, Devi thought.

"Stop it! Stop it now!" Wanda commanded.

"Stop it, what?" asked a startled Devi.

"I see that look in your eye. I know what you're thinking, but my girl had gotten clean. She wasn't doing those things anymore. They killed her because she was about to blow this town wide open."

"What do you mean?"

"I mean she was about to expose all the corruption that goes on here. The drug dealing, the abuse of power, the embezzlement, the killings, all of it. Every bit of it."

Devi was overwhelmed by what she heard. She glanced at the clock at saw it was barely six fifteen- way too early for this kind of information, she thought.

"Wanda…what?"

"You heard me. That commissioner Pug Cain? He's the leader of the pack. My girl was dating his son so she had proof of it all."

Pug Cain? The same County Commissioner Pug Cain that Devi had sat next to at the Rotary meeting? The same Pug Cain who gave Devi his number and told her to call him if she needed anything at all? He was so, well, charming. Wanda must be mistaken, Devi thought.

"Wanda, what do you mean when you say proof?"

"Before I tell you, you have to promise me one thing."

"What's that?"

"You'll investigate these jack-rabbits and do a story on it to expose them. I want them to all rot in prison."

"Yes, of course. Allison was my cousin and I loved her dearly. If someone did something to her, of course I'll expose them," Devi said from the bottom of her heart.

Wanda inhaled deeply and let it out slowly. She wanted to make sure she left nothing out. She also didn't want to sound like the loon people always accused her of being. She decided to just start with the beginning. Well, Allison's beginning.

"After your Uncle Clem passed away and we moved up here, as you can imagine, Allison was still pretty distraught. Depressed even. They never found Clem's body. The police just came and told us he had been lost at sea on a fishing trip he was on, but we never got to say our proper goodbyes. No closure. So Allison got started with all kinds of drugs."

Devi squinted and gave Wanda the side eye. Wanda knew full well Allison was on drugs long before any move to Oregon or death of her father. Devi prepared herself to hear the rest of Wanda's fantasy laced tirade. Clearly she was delusional.

"Well, what I mean is she got hooked on more kinds of drugs. Truth be told that girl had been doing drugs since junior high."

Devi nodded her head in agreement.

"Anyway, she got hooked on all types of stuff up here, but what did her really dirty was the heroin. She was like a whole other person on that stuff. It got so bad I had to…"

Wanda took in another deep sigh and her hands began to shake. Devi placed her hand atop Wanda's in an attempt to comfort her. She looked Wanda in the eyes and silently begged her to go on.

"I had to put her out of the house."

Devi was shocked. Wanda and Allison had always been thick as thieves. They were literally two peas in a pod. Drugs or no, you had to admire to affection between them. Old Clem really loved his girls, but nothing beat the way his girls loved each other. Devi couldn't imagine a scenario where Wanda would put Allison out.

"Where did she go?"

"Well, the streets. At first, anyway. She did that for about ten months. Slept behind dumpsters and over on the side of the Walmart. I even got wind one time of her living at that homeless camp up by the waterfall."

Devi wasn't familiar with any of the places Wanda named, but the thought made her cringe. Despite her faults, Allison was still her cousin. They'd played together as little kids and shared dreams and aspirations. Allison didn't stand a chance, though. Two junkies raising a child with no intervention is a recipe for the child to turn out just the same, Devi thought. She looked sympathetically at Wanda.

"So, was she still on the street when she died?"

"No. She came by the doctor's office where I work one day and told me she wanted to go to rehab. So I sent her. Paid for the whole thing."

Devi looked stunned. First and foremost, she couldn't understand how Wanda was able to get a job, let alone at a doctor's office. She also couldn't understand how, if Allison went to rehab, she still wound up dead of an overdose. She needed the holes filled in.

"Then she came home? After rehab?"

"No. I sent her to the rehab and she ran off."

"What do you mean she ran off?"

"She ran off. She called me crying that night. She was telling me that she bought her dope from Pug Cain but while she was at the rehab she found out he owned it."

"Wait. He sold her drugs but also owned a rehab?"

"Yes."

"Go on."

"Well, she wasn't supposed to have her cell phone there and when they caught her with it, they told her she was going to have to do the police department some favors if they didn't want them to plant some false evidence on her and lock her in prison forever."

"Wait. I thought you said she ran off. How did they catch her with the cell phone? And so what if she wasn't at the facility?"

"No. She called me while she was still there. After they threatened her she got scared and stole a car and ran off."

"Stole a car?"

"Yeah. One of the nurses left their keys in their truck and she knew that. So she took it. She wasn't a thief, though. She was going to bring it back or call them to come get it. She was scared. She just wanted to get away before they killed her."

"Why did she think they would kill her?"

"Because she had the evidence."

"What evidence?"

"Well, I told you she was dating that Cain boy. He had given her a bag full of documents showing what was going on. That his daddy was the ring leader of all the bad stuff around here. She had mentioned in group therapy having it and so she just knew in her heart they found out and would kill her if they locked her up."

"What kind of documents?"

"I don't know. I just know not long after my girl turned up dead in a motel room and they laid blame to buprenorphine"

"But even if the commissioner guy is corrupt, why would that make the police kill Allison? Doesn't make sense."

"That's what I want you to find out. I got fifteen hundred dollars. I'll pay you to get the proof that they killed my girl and stole her baby," Wanda said as she fished the money out of her pocket.

"Baby?" Devi asked.

"Yes. I was keeping him because she wasn't fit anymore. The night they told me she died, someone came in my house and stole him. I saw the man leave with him. He carried him like a football down the hall and right out the front door."

"Did you report this to the police? What did they say? Are they still looking for him?" Devi quizzed Wanda.

"I think the police are the ones who killed my daughter. So, no! I sure didn't report it to them!" Wanda wailed as she extended a fist full of money toward Devi.

Devi eyeballed the money. Fifteen hundred dollars wasn't even close to what Wanda had begged or borrowed from her over the years. She didn't want the money, though. She wanted to know what really happened to her cousin. If Allison died of a drug overdose, that was one thing. If anyone truly did harm to her, Devi wanted blood. She tossed the scenario around in her head for a moment. The more she tossed it around, the more she became convinced Allison died of an overdose and there probably never was a baby.

"I don't want your money, Wanda, but I'll check into it, ok?"

"Good. Now tell me about this man of yours."
They both burst into a fit of giggles.

CHAPTER FIVE

It was Devi's first weekend in "The Burg" as some locals called it. She desperately wanted to go out for some enchiladas. There were none to be found, at least not to her liking. Against her better judgement, Devi decided to call Wanda for a suggestion. They agreed to go dutch and meet at Tia Juana's House of Mexico.

Three hours later and stuffed like teddy bears, Kolton and Devi returned home. As they pulled up in the driveway, Kolton noticed Shane wasn't home. He was about to make a sarcastic comment to his mother, but Devi's eyes said that she, too, observed Shane's absence.

"Well, looks like it's just you and me kid… again."

Devi sighed as she took her keys out of the ignition and motioned for Kolton to follow her into the house from the passenger seat. As they entered the house, it was eerily quiet. Normally, you could at least hear the hum of the old refrigerator in the kitchen. But it was dead silent tonight. Devi felt for the light switch as she paused Kolton behind her.

She found it and nimbly flipped the switch. Nothing.

"What is it?" Kolton asked.

Devi motioned for him to be quiet. It was at that moment that a shadowy figure moved toward them. Preemtively, Devi charged forward, spun, kicked, then swept the figure's feet from beneath him. He snapped back to his feet like a bungie cord, hurling blows toward Devi's face. Beads of sweat formed on her upper lip as she ducked and dodged. Kolton, despite the shakiness in his limbs, hurled every object he could get his hands on in the dark toward the intruder.

The figure aimed a vicious round-house kick toward Devi's face. She swung and unleashed a flurry of attacks in response, which resulted in the figure's face mask coming off. The now unmasked man sprinted toward the patio door. Devi threw a lamp toward him.

"Is that all you've got?" he turned around to taunt.

"No. It's not," Devi calmly replied before she grabbed a sword from a wall display.

She pulled the sword back, ready to drive it through the man's skull. He ducked, then escaped through patio door, into the woods. Devi relaxed as she dropped the sword to the ground. Kolton ran to her side.

"Are you ok? I'm calling nine-one-one!"

He reached in his pocket for his phone, but it wasn't there. Devi pulled her phone out of her purse, still on her shoulder, and handed it to him. It rang and startled them both. It was Wanda.

"You talk to your crazy family," Kolton said as he tossed the phone back to Devi.

She explained what happened and Wanda promised to run right over. Devi hung up and surveyed the damage of the room. The scene was what Devi imagined it must look like if there was an explosion in a glass factory.

Kolton piddled around in the kitchen and then returned with a broom to sweep up the mess.

"I don't know if he cut the power lines or the fuse blew, but let me get some lights on in here," Devi declared before she stood up.

"It's not a fuse," Kolton relayed. "I already looked. The box is in the kitchen."

Devi groaned aloud. This was more excitement than one person should have, she thought. She decided to let Shane handle it when he came home. In this tiny town, he was some kind of VIP or something, she chuckled, so maybe the electric company would respond more quickly if he placed the call. She glanced at her watch. It was a quarter til nine. Who worked that late on a Saturday night at a VA hospital, she wondered.

The knock at the door startled them both.

"It's me! Wanda! Y'all all right in there?"

Devi ushered her guest in. They hugged. Devi told her about the attack a second time. Wanda seemed to stare off into space.

"Wanda? Do you hear me talking to you? We could have died tonight and you're just sitting there giving me a deer in the headlight look. Are you high are something? You told me you weren't doing drugs anymore!" Devi was disgusted.

"No, hon. It's that picture over there on the mantle. Is he the fella who owns this house? YOUR fella?"

"Who cares, Wanda? I almost died!"

"Well, I care. He's the one who stole my grandboy."

"I knew I didn't like him," Kolton said to nobody in particular.

"Aunt Wanda! Enough! I don't know what is going on, but Shane-"

"Runs the local VA hospital. He let me know just how much weight his voice carries and how little mine does around here."

Devi narrowed her eyes and rubbed her temples.

"When was this?" Devi wearily asked, as Kolton moved closer so he could hear the conversation better.

"When he and his gang stole my grandboy!"

"I thought you said the sheriff stole the baby?"

"She ordered it, but he did it."

"You sound like a crazy person, Aunt Wanda. Shane is retired from the military, runs a hospital and works at his church. Why would he be out stealing babies?"

"I, well, I don't know. You think I made up a man breaking in here tonight, too?"

Devi released a heavy sigh before she answered a terse "no."

"Then will you help me find out who killed my daughter and who took her baby? And help me send them all to hell?"

"No!" Kolton blurted out. "I want to go home, not play detective."

Devi gives Kolton a quick hug.

"I want to go home, too. First, though, I want to get all the interviews I need for this story on that explosion. As soon as I do, we're out of here."

"I told you. I'm your ride or die. But I prefer to ride and not die."

Devi smiled faintly and turned her attention toward Wanda.

"Aunt Wanda, go home. I'll let you know what I decide. In the meantime, call the state police about the baby."

"No. I don't trust any of 'em. I'll go look for him myself," Wanda says as she turns to leave.

"No!" Devi commands. "Go home and stay there. Let me check a few things out."

"So, you'll help me?"

"I didn't say that…"

"Fine!"

Wanda storms out and Devi flops down on the sofa in the dark while Kolton continued to pick up the mess around them.

"I want to go home, Mom."

"We will. As soon as I figure out what is going on. Come on. We're going for a ride."

With that, Devi sprung to her feet and made a beeline for the door.

CHAPTER SIX

Devi's pick-up truck came to a stop in front of Ben Johnson's house. Kolton looks at the passenger window toward the house. The grass hadn't been cut in decades, while the wooden framed abode seemed to have been neglected for even longer. A dog yowled from the back, no lights were on, and a lone man sat in his boxers and an undershirt on the front porch. His nearly three hundred pound frame suffocated the rocker in which he sat. He sat motionless except to wave an old newspaper as a fan periodically.

"I'm good. I'll wait here," Kolton let Devi know after her surveyed the scene.

"That's fine. I'll be right back."

Devi stopped at the edge of the yard. She ignored the flutter in her belly and called out to the man on the porch.

"Mr. Johnson? It's Devi. I called you a little while ago about the blast. Thanks for seeing me so soon."

"Well, you were already out driving. Come on and have a seat. My wife just went to bed, but I'm a night owl. Well, what do you want to know about the blast? As I was a firefighter, I can tell you a heap!"

"I want to hear it all. But first, I'd like to ask you about another incident."

"What incident might that be?"

"There was a woman found overdosed in a motel a few weeks ago."

"Yep. I heard about that. So? We have plenty of junkies overdosing every single day. That's not a story. That blast is, though."

"Lots of people die from drug overdoses here?"

"Tons. Ever since they legalized darn near every drug known to man, the deaths have gone through the roof."

"Every drug known to man?"

"Let's see. Mary-Juana. Then there's cocaine, heroin. Uhm, magic mushrooms. A few other things…"

"These things are legal in Oregon?"

"Well, decriminalized, but they may as well be legal. You don't even get so much as a slap on the wrist anymore."

"What *do* you get?"

"A thirty day stay over to the drug rehab facility for a second chance. Or an eighty third chance. Unlimited chances. Most of these folks have had a million second chances by now."

"Interesting. When did they decriminalize?"

"About a year ago. You know, you should really talk to Karen Weems over at the diner. She was compiling some stats."

Devi hops up.

"I sure will, Mr. Johnson! Thank you!"

She turns and sprints toward her truck.

"What about the blast?" he calls after her.

Devi had already started her engine and was barreling away, as fast as she could.

"Can we go home now?" Kolton asked.

"Not yet. Quick stop at the diner first."

"I thought you hate their food? Too greasy."

"Well, tonight, I'm not after their food. I just need some insight."

Kolton wasn't sure he wanted to know what that meant, so he just sat silently until they reached their destination. As Devi climbed out of her vehicle, she motioned for Kolton to follow. He grudgingly did so.

A scant crowd filled the diner. A waitress pointed Devi toward a table. Another waitress met her at the table and handed Devi a menu. Devi read her name tag. It said KAREN.

"Good evening, Ms. Karen. I'd like an order of hot cakes to go, but a coffee for here, please," Devi announced as she bit her lip with cautious hope.

"And I'll take a burger with provolone and bacon," Kolton added.

"You got it!"

The waitress pivoted to walk off. Devi grabbed her wrist. Karen eyeballed Devi.

"I was wondering if I could talk to you about the number of overdose deaths here in this town lately," Devi whispered as she released her grasp.

"Yes, m'am. I can add that to your order. Extra butter with those hotcakes. Got it."

Karen walked away as Devi turned her attention to her phone. She picked a game and enthusiastically played. Kolton was also engrossed in his phone for a moment. A third waitress brought Devi's coffee. That's when Kolton noticed the man in uniform at the next table. He kicked Devi under the table.

"What was that for?"

Kolton leaned his head in the direction of the other table. The man openly stared at Devi. He stood up and made his way toward her.

"I haven't seen you around here before."

"No. I'm new."

"You'll find that locals aren't too partial to strangers. What's your name?"

Devi's eyes turned toward his nametag. RENNICK.

"M'am. My name is m'am, deputy Rennick."

"Oh. You're a wise one, are you?"

"No. I'm a writer, actually."

Karen approached with impeccable timing. She handed Devi two Styrofoam containers. Then she gave Deputy Rennick an icy glare.

"I can cash you out over here, Samuel. Do you need a refill on your coffee, m'am?"

"No. How much do I owe you?"

"Not a thing. That gentleman over there took care of it."

The spot where she pointed was empty.

"I guess he left. Well, have a good rest of your night!"

Devi glanced at the deputy again on her way out. He gestured that he would have his eyes on her. Devi laughed and made her way to her truck and hopped in. She was a little perturbed the waitress ignored her request for information, but she decided to approach her on another day when the diner wasn't as busy.

"Now can we go home?" Kolton pleaded as he buckled his seat belt.

"Not yet. I have a wee bit more fact finding to do. This may very well pan out into another story after all."

Kolton then opened one of the Styrofoam containers as Devi put the truck in gear and drove away from the diner.

"What the heck?"

Devi glanced over at Kolton. He held up a mound of crinkled papers in one hand and an old cell phone in the other.

"Read it. What's it say? What is all that?" Devi barked.

Kolton sifted through the papers. He read them aloud:

"So you are the infamous Devi. Word of you spread through town like wildfire yesterday. I was hoping you'd visit."

Kolton and Devi exchanged a glance. He continues to read:

"As you'll see when you review these statistics, nearly ten percent of our town has dropped dead from an OD since they legalized so many drugs."

"Decriminalized," Devi corrected.

"Huh?" Kolton was confused.

"Go on. Keep reading," Devi urged.

"You will also find it interesting that the same week they legalized the drugs, one of our county commissioners, Pug Cain, opened four drug rehab facilities. The very same week! I put two and two together, but no one will listen to me because they are all in on it. They are shoveling dope into the veins of our residents, getting them addicted, then getting richer by charging their state health insurance for rehab fees. The cycle just repeats itself over and over and over. Someone has to put a stop to it. I heard you are some kind of detective writer or…"

"Investigative journalist," Devi corrected.

"Huh?"

"Kolton, keep reading!" Devi demanded, as she pushed her foot a little deeper into the gas pedal.

"I heard you are some kind of detective writer or something. I sure hope you can look into all of this. It might help you to talk to Fred Summers over at the mill. He's on shift right now. Fred knows everything. EVERY. STINKING. THING. His number is in the burner cell."

"Is she talking about that old phone in the container?" Devi asked.

"Yep."

"What else is in the box?"

"Well, definitely not a burger with provolone," Kolton said as he sifted through the papers again. "It's a bunch of people's names with phone numbers, some news clippings talking about decriminalizing drugs and a key."

"A key?"

Kolton held up the key.

"Does it say somewhere in all that stuff what it goes to?"

Kolton sifted through everything again. He held up a sheet of paper, then tossed it aside before declaring that there was no information on what the key opened. In response, Devi pulled over in a gas station parking lot. She pulled out her phone.

"Mom, what are you doing?"

"I'm looking up directions to the mill. Maybe Fred Summers can tell me what that key goes to and why I have it.

"

Devi turned her attention back to her phone as Kolton stared out the window.

"Hey, is that sheriff guy following us?"

"What sheriff guy?"

"Over there. The guy from the diner."

Devi looked out the passenger side window. Rennick waved.

"Here. Take my phone. Let's get out of here."

They drove in silence for a few miles.

"Turn right at the stop sign," Kolton read from her phone.

Devi turned right, but looked in her rear view mirror.

"Don't worry. He's not following us anymore," Kolton proclaimed.

Devi smiled.

"Turn right, and then?

"And then, according to this, your destination is on your left one mile down."

They rode in silence for a few minutes.

"There it is. I see it!" Devi excitedly shared.

Devi pointed to a sign that read SUMMERS LUMBER MILL. She pulled into the dirt parking lot, turned off the truck, and stared at the floor.

"What's wrong?" Kolton asked.

"I'm debating if I should call and have him come outside, or just go in and find him."

"Please do whichever one will get us home faster."

Devi dialed the number listed on the sign. The phone is answered on the first ring.

"Is Mr. Fred Summers in tonight?"

She nodded to Kolton and mouthed "It's him."

"Yes, that's right. My name sure is Devi. I was wondering if we could chat for a little bit? I'm actually outside the mill now."

She paused for a moment, but Kolton couldn't hear what was being said on the other end of the line.

"Ok. Sounds good. See you then."

Devi tossed her phone to Kolton and started the truck.

"What did he say?" Kolton asked.

"He said he would love to talk, but not here. He'll meet me at the T-Mart parking lot in a few minutes, by the front door."

She put the truck in reverse, backed up, then abruptly stopped. She saw a billboard. It had a huge photo of Pug Cain with the slogan "Umqua Valley's Savior." Davi shuddered, then drove away.

CHAPTER SEVEN

Devi pulled into the fire lane near the front door of the T-Mart. It was closed for the day, so no one would mind. T-Mart was a sad Walmart knock-off, that looked even sadder in the moonlight. A few minutes passed before a green van backed into place next to her, window to window. The driver, Fred Summers, rolled his window down.

"Miss Devi? Is that you?"

"In the flesh."

"How can I help you?"

"Well, Karen tells me you know everything. I'd love to know more about how drugs are impacting people around here."

"Around here, or over at the hospital?"

Devi leaned in. Fred had her attention.

"At the hospital?" she asked.

"Well, that's where most of the trading back and forth takes place."

"Really…"

"Yes, really. It got so bad at one point, my cousin Jimmy who is head of maintenance over there told me he almost lost his job."

"He got addicted?"

"Oh, heavens no. One of the head honchos was having Jimmy order furniture on the hospital's dime, then selling it out the back door. He'd take that money and buy large sums of all kinds of dope."

"That's crazy! A head honcho of what hospital?"

"Liberty VA Hospital."

Devi and Kolton made eye contact with each other.

"I knew I didn't like that guy," Kolton declared, loudly enough for Fred to hear.

Devi pinched Kolton's leg, then resumed her conversation with Fred.

"Do you know the head honcho's name, by any chance?"

"Uhmm, let me think a minute. Steven. No wait. Shane. Shane Gaebler."

"You don't think Jimmy is mistaken about this, do you?"

"No way. Everyone in this town knows what a louse that Gaebler guy is."

Kolton gave Devi a side eyed look, which she pretended not to see.

"I see. Well, why would a hospital administrator be buying drugs, at work, no less?"

"Why does he do any of the corrupt stuff he does? Raping women. Threatening people's jobs if he doesn't get his way. He's a demon."

"I'm so ready to go home," Kolton mutters to no one in particular.

"If all of this is going on, how does he keep his job?"

"That's the million dollar question," Fred said.

His phone rang. After a brief moment, he turned his attention back to Devi.

"That's the Mrs. I'm going to have to run for now. I'm using her van. She's a little nervous to have it out here for this meeting. Check in with Mike Flowers if you want more details."

"About Shane?" Devi queried.

"About the drugs being sold at the hospital. Mike's wife used to work for Shane. He can tell you more."

"How do I find him?"

"This town's small. You'll find him. Check on social media. He's on all the info groups for this town."

Fred waves as he backs up his van and departs.

"Rapes women. What else do you need to hear. Let's go home," Kolton urged.

Devi stayed silent as she slowly backed up to leave. In her rear-view mirror, she saw Rennick pull in behind her truck. He got out and walked to the driver's side window of Devi's truck.

"We just keep running into each other, don't we…m'am," Rennick growled, with heavy emphasis on the "m'am."

Kolton watched but stayed silent.

"Something I can help you with, deputy?" Devi asked, perturbed.

"Nope," Rennick said as he spat out a wad of tobacco and walked back to his patrol car. He jumped in and flipped his sirens and lights on. In a flash, he was no more than a blur that sailed down the road.

"That dude is a straight up weirdo," Kolton said.

Devi remained silent. She took in all that she had just heard about Shane. As she left the parking lot, she saw Fred Summers across the street at the hardware store parking lot, talking to three men. He pointed in her direction as she passed.

"I really just want to go home," Kolton sighed.

"Soon. I promise."

Devi looked at her watch. It was almost midnight. She pressed the gas pedal a little harder. She wanted to get back to Shane's place. She had questions.

It only took a few minutes and they were back at their temporary home. As they walked in, Shane greeted them from the sofa where he played his guitar.

"Hello, Beautiful! Did you have a good day?"

He rose to give Devi a peck on the cheek. Kolton snickered and headed to his room.

"What's with him? What's so funny?"

"Nothing. You know how young people are. We're *old* and everything we say or do is funny to them."

"I guess. Did you get some info on that story about the blast? You guys were out pretty late."

"Yeah, I interviewed a few people. You were out pretty late, too, though."

Shane ignored her question and plopped down on the couch again. He played his guitar as Devi sat in the arm chair across from him. She fished her computer out of her bag and looked up Mike Flowers on social media. She found him almost immediately.

She sent him a short note to request a meeting. He responded instantly. The agree to speak by phone at two o'clock the next day. He messaged his number. Devi replied by sending hers. Then she set an alarm on her phone for the meeting.

"I had a pretty tiring day. I'm going to bed."

"I won't be up too much longer, myself. What'd you get into that made you tired? Did you guys finally go on that hike you were talking about?"

"No. It just took a ton of energy fighting off the ninja that got into the house earlier today."

Shane stopped mid-strum on his guitar.

"The what?"

"The ninja. We battled it out and he left."

"Someone came in the house?"

"Yep. You didn't see the mess? And the power to the house was cut, too."

Shane looked hard and long before he said "I saw some glass in the trash. I thought maybe you broke a plate or something. The fuse was blown, but I replaced it. But as long as you are all right, that's what matters."

"I'm fine. I don't know about him, though.'

Shane played his guitar again.

"That's odd, " Devi observed.

"What's odd?"

"Your reaction."

"You said you were ok. What else do you want me to say?"

"Nothing. I'm going to lie down now."

"We'll go out for a nice dinner tomorrow and you'll forget all about that ninja. Probably just kids, though."

Devi laughed and made her way to bed. The next morning, Devi awoke to a note from Shane that he'd be at work most of the day, despite it being Sunday. Her first instinct was to call him. She snatched her phone off the nightstand and saw she had twenty six missed texts from Mike Flowers. They all said the same thing. "Call now please."

Devi dutifully dialed his number. Straight to voicemail. She dialed twice more. Same thing. She was puzzled.

"Hmmmm. That's strange."

Devi grabbed her laptop and visited the social media group to message him. She gasps and read snippets of the top post out loud:

"Spying for the hospital? Hired by Shane Gaebler? What on earth? I've been called many things, but never a spy!"

Her thoughts are interrupted when her phone rings. The caller ID says UNKNOWN CALLER. She quickly answered.

"Hello. Mr. Flowers?"

It's not Mr. Flowers. She is caught off guard. She hears light breathing on the other end. A woman greets her.

"Who is this?"

"My name is Tameka Blakely. I saw the messages on the town rants and raves page. I wanted to share some information."

She had Devi's attention.

"I'm listening, Ms. Blakely."

"Shane is bad news. Get away from him as fast as you can."

"Mind telling me more?"

"I used to work for him. When I wouldn't go out with him, he fired me."

"That's illegal."

"Not in this one horse town. If you are in a position of power here, it's all about stomping on the little guy."

"Labor laws are federal," Devi reminded her. "Why didn't you fight that?"

"I did for a while. But he destroyed everything that mattered to me. He is friends with my landlord at the time, so he even got me evicted."

"What! How? They have to have a reason. They can't just put you out."

"The reason was Shane Gaebler told him to. I found out later that he was selling dope for Gaebler, too."

"What?"

"Yes. At the hospital. Gaebler was liquidating furniture for cash and turning it into dope. My landlord was his delivery guy."

"Delivery guy?"

"Yes, delivery guy."

"How do you know Shane was involved with the drugs and not someone else."

"Because I saw it with my own two eyes. He invited me over to his house under false pretenses and I saw."

Devi pondered this revelation.

"Devi, look in the drawer where he keeps his guitar picks. It has a false bottom. You'll find drugs and more."

"More?"

"Naked pics of the sheriff. A list of women's names. Not sure what that's about. And drugs."

"Naked pics of the sheriff? He dated her?"

"Not that I know of. Her ex-husband put them out all over the internet. I guess Gaebler printed them out. He's a pervert."

"Sounds like it…"

"Did you know he lost custody of his son?"

"No. He told me eric was visiting his grandparents. That's not true?"

"When that kid was two years old, Shane beat the tar out of him so bad that the State intervened and took away his parental rights."

"What!"

"Yes. He hasn't seen him since, as far as I know."

"He told me he has been a single parent all these years. Said his son was on vacation with the grandparents so my son could stay in his room while we are here."

"He's been on vacation for twenty years or so then."

Devi heard footsteps.

"Can I call you back? I think I may have company," Devi whispers.

"Sure, doll. I'll text you my number."

Devi disconnected the call and threw herself into bed. There's a knock at the door.

"Come in!" she says as she sat up and feigned sleepiness.

"I was just checking to see if you were all right. I thought I heard voices."

"I talk in my sleep sometime."

"Oh, ok, well instead of dinner, you want to go eat an early lunch. I'm done working."

"Yeah, sure. Let me get dressed."

Within a half hour, Devi, Shane and Kolton occupied a booth at Laney's Country Kitchen. Kolton stared at his food, while Devi picked at hers. The color had been boiled out of the green beans. They were some shade of grade, but not an appetizing one. No salt, pepper or other season had been applied to the meat or pasta. They couldn't stomach the thought of actually putting this in their mouths. Shane, on the other hand, shoveled his food into his mouth at a high rate of speed.

"I take it you haven't eaten in a month or two," Devi chided Shane, and they all laughed.

"Feels like it. My day was just long. Made me super hungry," Shane said as he scarfed down more food.

Kolton's stomach turned as he watched this.

"So, yesterday was pretty interesting," Devi shared.

"You got a lot of research done?"

"She got a lot of research done, all right," Kolton remarked.

Devi kicked him under the table. Shane crammed more food into his mouth before he spoke.

"My grandpa has some stories to tell about that blast. I'll give you his number."

"Cool. Thanks. Hey…do you know Mark Flowers?"

"No. I don't know anyone with that name."

Kolton excused himself from the table. He headed toward the bathroom, almost in a dead sprint. He wanted no parts of the conversation that was to come.

"Really? He knows you pretty well. In fact, he seems to despise you."

"Me? Why?"

"I don't know. I had an interview planned with him but he cancelled at the last minute."

"Because of me?

"Yeah. Basically said he hates your guts. You are the devil and if I am involved with you on any level, I must be, too."

"I don't even know who he is."

"His wife never worked for you?"

"Who is his wife?"

"Leigh Anne Flowers?"

Shane paused mid-shovel of food to his mouth. He let his fork fall to his plate. He squinted and gave Devi a look of annoyance. His expression grew cold and he winced before he answered.

"She didn't work for me. As I recall, she fell asleep on duty and I had to approve her termination."

"Oh, I see. I guess that's why you've been deemed the devil then."

Devi scooted further apart from him in their booth and watched as he shoveled more food into his mouth. Silence filled the air for a few awkward moments .

"I wouldn't worry about them too much. He probably doesn't even have anything to contribute about the blast. I don't even think he was born yet."

"You're likely right, but I have another question for you."

Shane put his fork down and leaned back. He made no attempt to hide his annoyance. Devi took note of this before she spoke.

"When is your son coming home?"

"I need to call his grandparents. He should be home soon, though. A few weeks, probably."

Devi played with her food. She began to sweat.

"I was hoping to meet him."

"You will. I'll call his grandmother."

He paused and held his gut.

"I think I ate too fast. I'll be back. Need to visit the restroom," he shared before he pointed and left. His phone remained on the table. It had no password. Interesting, for a bad guy, Devi thought. She peeked in the direction of the bathroom to make sure he was inside. When she confirmed he was, quickly picked up the phone and scrolled through the photos. There were only selfies.

She then hurriedly scrolled through his contact list. She stopped when she reached her name. It reads *DEVI ALIBI*. She saw Kolton out of the corner of her eye and put the phone down.

"Worst food ever, Mom. Also, worst town and worst people ever. Are we ready to pack our things and go home yet?"

"Not just yet. Almost. Something is going on and I want to know what. I'm not leaving without all the pieces of this puzzle."

Kolton rolled his eyes. Shane was back. He plopped into the booth next to Kolton and across from Devi. He fidgeted for a moment.

"What's wrong?" Devi queried, full of fake concern.

"Nothing. Just ready to go. Are you two done?"

Devi looked at her plate and grabbed her purse. Kolton follows.

"Now it's my turn to use the bathroom. I'll be right back. Kolton, hold my purse."

Devi pitched her purse to her son and speed walked toward her destination. As she passed one of the tables near the bathroom, a woman handed her a note. Devi didn't break her stride. She continued to beeline for the bathroom. She exhaled hard when she got there. She leaned against the sink and looked in the mirror.

"Girlfriend. What are you doing?" she asked her reflection.

She stared at the paper in her hand for a moment before she uncrumpled it. There was a phone number on it., and a name: REID HANSHAW.

CHAPTER EIGHT

Shane, true to form, stretched out across the couch and fell into a deep slumber when they arrived home from the restaurant. Devi hid in the bedroom. She stroked the sheet of paper the woman gave her at the restaurant. She finally picked up her phone and dialed.

"Mr. Hanshaw? His, this is — (pause). Yes. I can meet you at the ice cream shop. Ten minutes. Got it. I'll be there."

She stuffed her phone in her pocket, grabbed her keys and headed to Kolton's room. She gently pushed his door open. He played a video game. Devi was glad she had not awakened him.

"Hey, Bud. Come take a ride with me."

"I thought you'd never ask. Who are we finding dirt on now?" Kolton teased.

Devi signaled him to be quiet. They giggled as they tip-toed out of the house to Devi's pick up truck.

"You know, maybe that deputy guy isn't so crazy after all. We are pretty easy to spot, you know. We stick out like sore thumbs."

Devi was puzzled. She cocked her head to one side.

"You're probably the only hot pink extended cab truck within a thousand miles of here."

They both broke out into a hushed laughter before they hopped in and drove away.

"Did your aunt call the sheriff about the baby?"

"I sure hope not."

"What do you mean you hope not?" Kolton said with air quotes.

"Something strange is going on here. It might not be safe to call them, Kolton."

"Why do you say that?"

"Just my gut. We have to figure out what's going on."

"We?"

"Yes. We."

They drove in silence for a few minutes before they arrived at Connie's Ice Cream Shack. A lone black car was parked in the lot. A man leaned against the trunk. It was their man. Devi exited the truck and walked toward Mr. Hanshaw. She stuck out a hand and he shook it.

"Call me Reid," he instructed.

"Ok, Reid. Call me Devi. How can I help?"

"You're a reporter, right?"

"Investigative journalist for a magazine…"

"Same thing. Well, everyone's tongue is wagging in this town about you."

"Is that so?" Devi said with a still demeanor as she observed Reid.

"That's so."

They stared uncomfortably at each other for a moment. Kolton, still in the passenger seat of the truck, caught his mother's attention when we suddenly motioned for her to look down the road. Rennick was back. This time, he perched across the street and watched. Devi saw him. She acknowledged his presence with a nod to Kolton.

"Well, how can I help you, Reid?"

"You've got that twisted. I'm going to help you. Here you go."

He tossed her a small black backpack. The dollar store variety.

"What's this?" Devi asked.

"Evidence."

"Evidence of what?" she asked as she unzipped the bag. Inside was a tape recorder. She hit play. A man spoke.

"Buprenorphine is the perfect tool. A standard tox screen won't detect it and it does the job perfectly."

Now a woman interjected on the recording.

"But how do we know how much to use?"

The man spoke again.

"It really doesn't matter. Just keep juicing them up til they pass out."

The woman hesitated before she spoke again.

"What if we kill them?"

"Don't worry. It's not that kind of drug. You literally can't overdose on it. But if they do, they're just meth heads. Isn't that right, Alley Cat?"

A second woman screamed. The two burst into laughter. Devi stopped the recording.

"Who is this?" she demanded.

"Our sheriff is one. Not sure who the others are."

"Who are they drugging? And how did you get this?"

"That's all you. I brought you evidence that they are doin' somethin' shady. Now you research it and find out what."

He hopped back in his vehicle and sped away down the winding road to the east. Devi looked in the bag. There was a gaggle of papers. On top was a note. It said "Call Luca Sherman. He wants to talk." Conveniently, Luca's phone number was written on the note. Devi stuffed everything back into the bag and turned toward her truck.

When she reached it, she tossed the bag to Kolton as she got in the driver's seat. She looked in her rear-view mirror. Rennick waved from his spot across the road. Devi inhaled deeply, then exhaled slowly. She and Kolton jumped like scared cats when her phone rang in the next moment.

"Hello? (pause) Aunt Wanda? (pause) I believe you. Do not call the sheriff. (pause) I'm going to find your grandson. I promise."

She hung up and high-tailed it back to Shane's house. She whispered for Kolton to be quiet as they entered the front door. They both rolled their eyes when they saw him still sprawled in the same spot where they left him earlier.

"Follow me," Devi whispered to Kolton. They tip-toed downstairs to the basement where Shane's home office was. Devi told Kolton to guard the door. Kolton looked around for a moment, then grabbed a nearby pvc pipe that was propped against the wall. Devi nodded approval, then disappeared into the office.

She rummaged for a few moments, unsure of what she was looking for. She opened the bottom desk drawer. Inside was a box. She decided it needed to be opened. Once she did so, all she could do was stare.

"Who in the world has an entire box full of wedding bands?" she wondered aloud.

She whipped out her phone and snapped a photo. Then she carefully replaced the box. Kolton leaned his head into the room.

"Hurry up before he wakes up."

"He won't. He had way too much to eat at that rotten restaurant."

"Well, hurry anyway," Kolton pleaded. "What are you even looking for?"

Devi thought for a split second.

"I don't know yet. I'll know when I find it."

She closed her eyes before she spoke again.

"Look in the drawer where he keeps his guitar picks. It has a false bottom. You'll find that and more."

"I'm not touching anything," Kolton declared.

"No, no. I was repeating what that woman told me on the phone. Where does he keep his guitar picks?"

Kolton pointed to the top desk drawer. Devi pulled but it was locked. She found a paper clip and was able to use it like a key to get in. She removed the contents, then the bottom. She leaned in.

"What?" Kolton asked, spooked.

"I'm not sure. What is this?"

She held up a baggie of what looked like cocaine. Then she withdrew a handful of filled syringes from the drawer. They were labeled BUPRENORPHINE. Devi took photos with her phone, then replaced everything.

"So he's a drug dealer. But what is with the syringes. Is he drugging people or drugging people so they use his drugs? None of this makes sense," Kolton said in a whisper.

"No. It doesn't."

Devi walked over to a filing cabinet and yanked a drawer open. Inside were stacks of cash. Her eyes bulged. Kolton zipped over and took a peek.

"Mom, seriously, let's get out of here."

"We will. We will. I promise."

Devi snapped a few more photographs. She opened another drawer of the filing cabinet. There was a list. She picked it up and read it aloud.

"Katy Stinnett. Anna Wiseman. Lollie Goodman. Allison Katrine."

Devi froze. She read the name again. She closed her eyes for a few seconds. When she opened them, she read the names aloud again.

"Katy Stinnett. Anna Wiseman. Lolli Goodman. Allison Katrine. Then it says one two four exit. What in the world does that mean?"

"One two four exit? Sounds like shorthand, but I don't know for what," Kolton chimed in.

Devi folded the paper and placed it in her bra.

"Let's get out of here, Kolton. I think we found all there is to be seen here."

Devi hesitated, Kolton did not. He bolted out the door and back up the stairs. When Devi finally left several minutes later, just as she closed the door, she turned around and was face to face with Shane.

"I was wondering where you were," he said as he kissed the top of her head.

"I thought you might have some cards laying around so I could play Solitaire. But, you don't," Devi said with a slight laugh.

"I haven't seen a deck of cards in years. Since my days in the Army."

"When did you retire? Was it before me or after?"

"I didn't retire," he said with a smirk.

"No? I could have sworn you told me you retired."

"Nah. I got kicked out. Drunk driving. Right after you left the unit actually."

"I could have sworn you said you retired."

Shane glanced at his office door just long enough to make Devi uneasy. She decided to end the confrontation and get far, far away from this louse.

"I think it's my turn for a nap, Shane. Wake me up in an hour, please," she said as she raced upstairs.

Shane watched her leave. He waited until she was gone to open the door to his office. He surveyed the area with the lights off. Nothing was out of place. He yawned and shut the door, then headed back upstairs.

Later that night, long after Shane was in bed, Devi snuck down the hall to Kolton's room. He was sound asleep with his head buried under the covers. She sat on the edge, next to him. She gently tapped him until he awoke, disoriented and blurry-eyed. Devi held up her phone.

"You never found your phone?"

"Nope. To be honest, I hadn't had a real chance to look. Ping it."

"What?"

Kolton took her phone and pressed some keys. Devi wasn't quite sure which ones. A moment later, his phone rang. They followed the sound. They tip toed down the hallway. The sound grew louder. It became even louder when they got to Shane's door. They froze. Kolton snatched Devi's phone and pushed a few buttons. The ringing stopped. They both breathed a sigh of relief. They run back to Kolton's room as noiselessly as possible. Kolton flung open the closet doors and started cramming clothes into a suitcase. He urged Devi to do the same. Instead, she made a phone call.

"Tameka? Hi, this is Devi. I am so sorry to call this late, but this is super important. I think I found something."

"To link him to the drugs? I told ya!"

"No. Worse. My dead cousin's name on a paper with the words one two four exit. Do you know if that is some kind of code?"

"One two four exit? Like, Exit one-twenty-four? On the freeway?"

"I have no clue, Tameka."

"That's where they say the entrance is to the underground city."

"What underground city?" Devi nearly screamed.

"Might be an urban legend, but they once found a severed head over that way."

Devi grimaced. She froze, as she heard footsteps.

"I'll call you back," she whispered to Tameka.

The footsteps paused. Devi froze in place and motioned for Kolton to do the same. Within seconds, they retreated. Devi exhaled silently. She whipped her phone out and dialed.

"Wanda? (pause) I may have some information about what happened to Allison. First, though, did they call her Alley Cat?"

"Ever since we moved up here. She wanted a new identity, so she shortened her first and middle names and came up with Alli Kat."

"Do you know anything about an underground city?"

"That's an old wife's tale. Doesn't exist."

"But what if it did? What sorts of things would I find there?"

"Trouble with a capital T. What are you on to?"

"I don't know. I will tell you in the morning. Any word on the baby?"

"I got every lumber jack I know in this county on the hunt for him."

"Good. Steer clear of the sheriff. You might be right about them all being corrupt."

"I know I'm right."

Devi told Wanda goodnight and ended the call. She pulled the recorder out of the black bag that rested on the foot of Kolton's bed. She hit play. She winced as she heard the man say

"Buprenorphine is the perfect tool. A standard tox screen won't detect it and it does the job perfectly."

She realized she recognized the voice.

"Well, I'll be darn!"

Kolton turns to face her, as he continued to pack.

"What?"

"That voice. It's Deputy Rennick."

She replayed the man speaking again. There was no doubt who it was this time.

"Can we please just get out of here?"

"Soon. I need to take a ride first. We'll finish this later. Come on."

Kolton rolled his eyes, but complied. Before long, they barreled down I-5 to exit 124, which happened to be where the diner was. Devi parked at the diner, then she and Kolton walked over to the freeway exit sign. They looked around. Fir trees. A forest animal or two. Then Kolton sees it.

"Mom, look. A door!"

They walk toward it. It was formed from iron bars.

"Murphy's Law. It's padlocked."

They both peer in.

"Hello! Anyone down there?" Devi yells.

"Are you nuts? Like the bad guys are just going to say yes, m'am! Come on down," Kolton mocked before he told her to be quiet.

They could hear a faint cry for help. Then multiple cries. Devi shook the door. It was obvious the cries were from women. The door didn't budge. Devi cursed, then looked around.

"What are you looking for?"

"A rock. Or something I can pound this lock off with."

"Wait. Remember that key the lady gave you this morning?"

"Now that would just be too much if that key goes to this lock."

"Let's try it."

Kolton sprinted back to the truck. He retrieved the key and was back in a flash. It was a match! They opened the door and then proceeded down a dirt staircase. Devi pulled her phone out for light. The distress cries went quiet. Devi shined her light to see her surroundings. A family of rats snarled, then scampered away. Devi falls back, aghast. She hated rodents.

In the distance, somewhere in the tunnel, they could hear footsteps. Devi turned off her light. They paused. The cries for help had begun again. Devi and Kolton continued to make their way toward the cries.

"This way," Kolton says with his pointer finger extended.

Devi followed. Kolton pointed to the right.

"BLAM! BLAM! BLAM!"

Bullets fly overhead. Devi's military instincts kick in. Without a second thought, she pushed Kolton down and ran toward the gunfire. With a running start, she kicked the shooter's weapon out of his hand. It landed near Kolton.

Kolton grabbed it. The shooter turned to run, but Kolton shot him in the leg first. The shot slammed the shooter against a dirt wall. He landed on his feet like a cat and charged Devi. She ducked, he landed on his face.

"Kolton, give me that gun!" Devi commanded.

Kolton tossed the gun to Devi. She straddled the shooter.

"Don't even think about moving or I'll end you."

The shooter stretches his arms upward, in defeat.

"Mom! Give me your phone! Turn the light on!"

At the moment Kolton illuminated the area, the shooter lunged at Devi.

"BLAM!"

One shot to the head and the threat is neutralized. Devi stepped over him, grabbed Kolton's hand and continued toward the cries for help. About a quarter mile further in, they see two women locked in a cage.

"We're going to help you," Devi shared with the disheveled women.

"Help the others. We're ok," one of the women responded.

"Others?"

Devi waved the phone light around. She saw no one. Kolton kept his gaze fixed on the shooter.

"They brought in six more women about a week ago," the woman said.

"…and kids. Young girls and a few boys," the other woman continued.

Devi stood. They were at the end of the tunnel and there was no one else.

"Who brough you here?" Devi asked.

"I don't know. I was drugged, I think."

"Well, I know, drugged up or not. It was Sheriff McKenna and her good Rennick," the second woman informed them.

"Sheriff McKenna? Are you sure?" Devi asked.

"Yes. I'd know her no matter how stoned I was."

Devi searched around for something she could open the lock on the women's cage with. She spotted an ammo can atop a filing cabinet. She opened it and found 2 large rings of keys inside. She frantically started trying keys in the lock. None of them worked.

"Stand back," Devi barked.

The women obeyed, and Devi shot the lock off.

"Jesus…" Kolton muttered.

"How do you know there are others?" Devi interrogated the women.

"They were with us until yesterday. Then they moved us. They said it was time for auction."

"Auction?" Devi asked, confused.

"They sell us to men from China and in turn, they get discount drugs. They sneak us up the freeway to the coast."

"Never to be heard from again. Then they say we ran away or some horse puckey like that. No one looks for us, so they get away with it."

"How do you know that's the plan?" Devi demanded to know.

"I've heard them talking, and Commissioner Cain is heading it all up. That's how they get us out of the country so easily. He pays off all the eyes that matter."

"How is that even possible?" Devi wondered to no one in particular.

"Mom!"

Devi turned her attention to Kolton. Shane had Kolton in a headlock.

"Run, ladies!" Devi commands.

They did as they had been told.

"Let him go, Shane!"

"I was kind enough to let you stay in my home and this is how you repay me?"

"Don't make this worse on yourself, Shane. Let Kolton go."

"Your mom and I just aren't the same people, Kolton. I'm all about live and let live, but she just can't mind her own business."

"Let him go, Shane. Kolton, chin to chest!"

"I had a crush on you from the first time I saw you. Did you know that?"

"One!" Devi shouted.

"You're going to count to ten and then I pee my pants or what" Shane mocked with a smirk.

"Two!"

"I'm not going to be able to let you leave here, Devi. I've got a good thing going and you are not going to ruin it for me."

"Three!"

Kolton lurched forward and thrusted his head between his legs. In the process, Shane flipped to the ground and landed on his back. Devi fires in Shane's direction.

"BLAM!"

Shane was about to bound up again when Devi kicked him in the chin and stood straddled atop him.

"Don't even think about it. Where are the others?" Devi asked.

"What others?"

"The other women! Where are they?"

"You mean the meth-heads? No one cares. That's the beauty of all this," Shane chuckled.

Devi kicked him in the mouth.

"Where are they?" Devi inquired again.

He smirked. Devi shot him in his foot and he cried out in agony.

"You're not smart enough to coordinate all of this. What's your cut of this?"

Shane stares at Devi before he answers.

"Ten percent."

"Who do you report to?"

Shane became silent. Devi kicked his face again. She shot him first in one arm, then the other. He wailed in agony.

"Help me drag him into this cage, Kolton."

They dragged him to the far corner of the cage.

"But there's no lock," Kolton noticed.

"It's ok. He won't be going anywhere. He's going to bleed out."

She cocked the gun and shot Shane in both legs.

"May you rot in hell," she whispered to Shane before she grabbed Kolton's hand and the pair left. They made their way at full tilt out of the underground city and back to the diner parking lot. They bolted to Devi's truck and both leaned against the passenger side door.

"How about we get some food to go and I call the FBI or someone to come blow this town apart?" Devi said, out of breath.

"Go ahead and get in the truck. I'll run in and get two sandwiches to go."

Devi nodded her head and climbed in the passenger seat. She closed her eyes for a moment. She was exhausted. It seemed to her as if all she did was blink, and Kolton was back.

"All they had ready was coffee. I didn't feel like waiting fifteen or twenty minutes for a sandwich that you and I both know will be horrible," Kolton said as he handed her a steaming cup through the window. She took a sip and closed her eyes again.

"Here we go again," Kolton whispered.

Devi opened her eyes and turned her attention to her window. It was Deputy Rennick. He walked over to her open truck window.

"Hey, deputy," Devi said in a snarky tone.

She extended her hand to offer him a taste of coffee, then feigned an accident and spilled it all over his thigh.

"Oops. So sorry."

"You idiot! That is assault of a peace officer! Your poured that all over my me on purpose!"

"It was an accident. Honest."

Kolton had already run around and jumped into the driver's seat. He got it started, threw it in gear, and the two sped away.

CHAPTER EIGHT

It was dusk when Devi and Kolton returned to Shane's house. Devi chewed her lip as they scanned for threats s after they pulled up in the driveway. Though the seemingly most dark and foreboding threat had been neutralized, Shane, they wanted to be sure nothing else lurked in the shadows. Kolton's heart pounded as Devi instructed him to very gently close his door so it wouldn't make any noise. Her belly was full of whatever was going on in this town and she wanted to head home…now.

"Grab whatever is left and drag it to the front door," Devi said in a low whisper.

"We can finally leave now?"

"We have a couple more things to do, then yes, we're out of here."

"You don't think he'll come back and start trouble do you?"

"Shane? No. He can rough-house with Satan, but he certainly won't be doing so with us or anybody else."

They entered the house and Kolton flipped the lights on. He and Devi both surveyed the living room. If they didn't know any better, they might think a happy little family lived there. Kolton headed to the bedroom to finish gathering his things. Devi pulled out her phone and stared at it for a moment. She took a deep breath and dialed.

"Wanda? It's Devi. Are those loggers still on standby? (pause) Good. I have a plan. If I call and tell you I have been arrested by the Sheriff, that's your cue to call my friend Ewen at the FBI and have him pounce on this house I am staying at. If I say I want all my friends to know, have the loggers assemble at this house I'm staying at."

"For what? What's going on?"

"Just trust me. Please. And write Ewen's number down. Two, zero, two, five, five five, seven, nine, six, two. (pause)"

Kolton walked in with an arm full of shoe boxes. He caught Devi's attention. He opened one and Devi's eyebrows furrowed. The box was full of cocaine and money. Devi did a double take and scratched her jaw. She swallowed hard before she returned to her phone conversation.

"Aunt Wanda, just trust me. The plan just got even better. Talk to you soon. I need to go."

Devi disconnected the call. A lump formed in her throat. Devi instructed Kolton to put all the shoe boxes he found in the front coat closet. He did as he was told, and within a few minutes, the closet was full from top to bottom of the shoe boxes. Devi didn't know who she was about to bring down, but she had satisfaction in knowing that someone's world was about to crumble. She grabbed Kolton's hand and told him everything would be all right. His mouth was dry and he felt sick, but he knew she told the truth. They looked around one last time before they made their way to Devi's truck.

Devi sped away as quickly as she could toward the main road. She wasn't quite sure what she would tell Tameka, but she knew she needed her help, so that was where she was headed. Devi had zero plans to stick around, but she knew she needed someone to make sure the head of this whole drug/human trafficking operation went down.

Devi dialed Tameka.

"This is Devi. I apologize for calling so late, but you won't even believe what I found! If it's all right, I'd like to head over to your place. We need a safe place to discuss all this. Can you text me your address?"

"Sure, my friend. Sending it now. See you in a few!"

Devi disconnected the call and concentrated on the road in front of her.

BLING!

Tameka had sent her address. Devi passed the phone to Kolton and had him read out directions to the address. They were there within four minutes.

"Wait here," she told Kolton as she hopped out.

Kolton reached over and locked the doors of the truck. He clenched his jaw as he thought of the dangers that might hide in the night. He had never hated trees before, but now they made him break into a sweat. He intended to take no unnecessary risks. He watched the house intently, and his heart raced. He began to sweat as the wheels of his imagination turned. Just when he was about to panic and bolt from the seat, Devi walked toward the truck. She entered her side, sighed heavily, then slammed the door shut.

"What happened in there? Why do you look so pissed?"

"Something just wasn't right. And watch your mouth."

Devi pulled the truck out of the driveway and made a right turn. A red car slid to a stop in front of her at that moment.

"Watch out!" Kolton yelled as he braced for impact.

Devi swerved to miss it.

"What the hell!" she screamed, as she craned her neck to get a look at the driver.

Another car swerved in front of them. Kolton's muscles tensed and his skin was clammy. He gasped for air. Devi's nostrils flared and her pulse raced as she skillfully evaded the car like a NASCAR driver. She watched in her rear-view mirror as the car sped off.

"Why the hell is everyone driving so crazy?" Kolton asked no one in particular.

"Watch your mouth… Doggone it! Look."

Devi pointed to the rear-view mirror. Kolton glanced up to see blue and red lights. He winced at the thought of what might be next. Devi's heartbeat thrashed wildly in her ears. The sirens erupted and they both knew that only meant more trouble.

"Please keep your mouth shut, Kolton."

"What's going on?"

"No idea, but we're about to find out."

Devi scanned the area, then decided to accelerate. The chase was on! She drove a short distance to an auto parts store.

As she reached it, she cut the corner into the parking lot too fast and her truck flipped. She sailed through the air like a bird.

The truck miraculously slammed down right side up. All the windows and windshield splintered into projectiles that filled the air like rain. The tires exploded, then the engine block dislodged. This knocked the hood wide open.

Devi and Kolton were bloody. As Devi attempted to remove her seat belt, the two cars that almost hit her earlier pulled in, along with two additional cars. Numerous deputies in full riot gear disembarked from the vehicles and surrounded Devi's truck with their weapons drawn.

"What do they want?" Kolton whispered as Devi grabbed his arm.

Devi could feel her body get weak, but she signaled to him to stop talking. She squinted and looked around. She noticed a woman in uniform walk toward them. When the woman, Jackie McKenna, who was built like a line-backer, reached the truck, she stood on Devi's side, with her weapon lodged squarely in the center of Devi's head. Samuel Rennick was on the passenger side of the truck with a weapon pointed at Kolton.

"Jackie McKenna, Sheriff! Get out of the vehicle and put your hands behind your neck!"

"Come on you gutter snipes! Get out of the car right now!" Sam Rennick added.

Devi scanned the area. She whispered to Kolton.

"What the hell? Don't do anything to provoke these people. They seem to be trigger happy."

Devi and Kolton raised their hands and opened the doors slowly. Tired of waiting, two deputies yanked them out and to the ground. Two more deputies grabbed Devi's arms, while a third grabbed her neck and bent her across the roof of the patrol car. Her face violently slammed into the roof. Her lip split and blood spurt every direction. The deputies snickered and handcuffed her. The same thing happened to Kolton on the other side of the car, but there was no split lip.

Sam Rennick let out a caterwaul.

"Finally some action in this pathetic town!" he cried with giddiness.

He walked toward his SUV. Jackie called over a female deputy. She instructed her to initiate a search of Devi, who was still face down across the roof of the patrol car. The deputy began with Devi's front pockets. Then her rear pockets.

"Well, well, what do we have here?" the deputy taunted as she held up a roll of large bills.

"Bingo!" mouthed Jackie McKenna with delight.

Devi, who was still face down on the car, strained to turn her head. She wanted to see what was going on, but she was held firmly in place by deputies. She scanned the sea of uniforms and spotted Sam Rennick. He walked toward her truck with a stuffed paper grocery bag. He placed the bag on the back seat of Devi's truck and left the door ajar.

"You son of a-- That's not mine!" Devi shrieked as adrenaline rushed through her body.

"It is now," he retorted with a smirk

Jackie McKenna walked and slammed the truck door shut. She gave Sam a pat on the back before she spoke again.

"We're done here, everyone. See you at the precinct," Jackie declared as she walked toward her own SUV and sped off.

Devi was separated from Kolton and this terrified her. Her nostrils flared and spittle built up in the corners of her mouth as she thought about what she'd do to them if they harmed a single hair on his head. Within a few minutes of placing her in the patrol car, they were downtown. They circled a five story building a few times before someone finally told them on the radio to bring the detainee to the back.

The car finally came to an abrupt halt on the bottom floor of a parking garage for the building. Jackie Mckenna snatched the door open and drug a handcuffed Devi to the elevator.

They rode the elevator in silence to the fourth floor. Devi stared at Jackie with contempt.

"How could you mistreat all those women? And why are you involved in the first place? You don't feel any shame?"

Heat rose behind Jackie's eyelids and a lump formed in her throat as she pretended not to hear. When they reached their destination, Sam Rennick greeted them. He grabbed Devi roughly and dragged her down the long hallway until they reached an open door. Devi saw Kolton. They made eye contact and she could tell he was shaken up, but all right. He was handcuffed to a chair.. A muffled confusion was heard behind Kolton. Rennick hovered over Devi for a moment. He savored her angst. Then he kicked the door shut.

He shoved her a bit further to the next room with an opened door. Then he tossed Devi into a chair that was reminiscent of the grade school chair/desk combination. Still in hand cuffs, blood oozed from Devi's facial wounds. Her skin was bruised and her clothes were blood soaked. Rennick pounded his fist on the desktop. He chuckled as he watched Devi recoil.

"You're going to be in prison until you're in your nineties. You'll be a shriveled prune when you get out!" he declared with a sense of superiority.

Then he kicked her chair. Devi glared at him for a long moment before she laughed menacingly.

"I'll be out before you know it, you abusive piece of trash," she calmly observed.

Rennick grabbed her by the throat.

"Shut up or I am going to show you what abuse is!" he growled.

With his free hand, he removed handcuff keys from his pocket. He dangled them in front of Devi's face. They brushed against her nose.

"Let me out of these handcuffs and I bet I'll show you what abuse is."

Rennick leaned in. He pressed his forehead to Devi's. Sweat and blood dripped from her face.

"Let's see what you've got," he said with a tinge of curiosity.

Kolton swore from the other room. Devi averted her eyes to his direction. The rooms adjoined and the door that separated them suddenly opened. It was Jackie.

She sauntered into the room. She dropped into a chair next to Devi.

"He has nothing to do with this," Devi pleaded, as a roiling heat rose in her belly

Rennick stood upright. He walked in Kolton's direction and slammed the door shut behind him. Devi heard Kolton yell:

"Don't touch me!"

Jackie shifted her body weight toward Devi.

"You have the power to stop all of this. Tell me who you work for, and where this money came from," Jackie beckoned.

"The money you planted in my truck? I've done nothing wrong. Believe it, or don't," Devi said as she felt her blood pressure rise.

Jackie stood. She took a step back and punched Devi square in the ear. Then she kneeled beside her.

"Shane. Remember him? He has told us most of what we need to know."

Devi responded with a glassy stare. She had a headache. Jackie spat on the floor and got to her feet. Devi watched for a brief moment, then hung her head as Kolton cried out again. The skin bunched around her eyes as she gave a pained stare in the direction of the sound. She felt nauseous. It hurt her soul to hear him wail like that.

"First of all, tell that jerk to stop antagonizing Kolton. Next, bring your boss here," Devi uttered with a pinched expression.

"And then?"

"And then I will talk to you about the real gold mine we both know you want. It's much more valuable than that phony junk you put in my truck."

Jackie stared at Devi. She spat again. Devi wrinkled her nose in revulsion at this. Jackie took her finger and swept her mouth, which caused a wad of tobacco to hit the floor. Devi turned her head away in disgust.

"Guys! Get in here!" Jackie yelled toward the others.

She grabbed a chair and scooted it near Devi. She positioned it so she could look her in the eyes. Jackie plopped down in the chair and leaned back, just as Sam Rennick and another deputy walked in.

"What's up?" he asked.

"My friend, tell them what you just told me."

"Let Kolton go and I'll tell you where the real gold mine is."

"Bull crap! She's screwing with us!"

"Do you really want to blow this opportunity? It could be this biggest thing this county has ever seen," Devi poked.

She felt overheated and light headed on the inside. On the outside, she exuded pure confidence and control.

"Why should we negotiate with you? All we have to do is get a warrant."

"And search where? You think I keep this in my truck? In my purse? Think again."

Sam and Jackie made uncomfortable eye contact. Jackie tapped her foot nervously before she spoke.

"Can you tell us everything we need to know? Who you work for and what they want?"

"Get Kolton some food, and I'll tell you what you need to know. And a tea. Get me a nice hot cup of tea, please."

Jackie laughed.

"Yeah, ok. I think we can do that. Give me a second to call this up the chain. Rennick, handle their catering order."

Jackie hopped up from her seat. She glanced at Devi for another split second before she left the room in a fit of laughter.

"Please just get Kolton something to eat. He hasn't had anything all day," Devi begs Rennick.

"I thought I'd get you your tea first, seeing how I'm already here. We have a coffee pot right over there. It'll only take me a second to get some hot water going."

Rennick walked over to the kitchenette behind Devi. He dumped out coffee from the pot before he rinsed it. As the water boils, he methodically took a coup out of the cupboard and walked it to Devi. He slammed it down on the desk.

"Do you want honey or sugar in your tea?" he asked.

Rennick retrieved the pot, which was full of hot water. He pours the water into the cup until it overflows. He then pushes the cup with the pot and turned the cup over. Hot water soaked Devi's leg and she screamed.

"You burned my leg!"

"Oops! I'm sorry."

His eyes began to tear up as he tried to hold back malicious laughter.

Jackie bursts into the room.

"What happened?"

"It was an accident, m'am. Wasn't it, Devi?"

"No. It was no accident! Keep this psychopath away from me or I'm not sharing any information with you."

"Move her cuffs to the front. Take her to the bathroom so she can check herself out for burns, you idiot!"

The second deputy, whom Devi had all but forgotten was even in the room, unlocked the handcuffs.

"He burned me on purpose!" Devi shouted to the room.

"You want me to call a doctor? But that might delay you getting home, though, Princess," Jackie McKenna said with a hint of delight at Devi's pain.

"Can I just call my Aunt? She's elderly and she will be worried. I was supposed to pick her up to go grocery shopping," Devi asked.

"Yeah, sure," Jackie responded.

"And my attorney?"

"Don't push your luck, Princess. But yeah, sure, that's fine," Jackie commented as she chewed gum much like a cow who chewed her cud.

Jackie pointed to the phone on the table, so Devi took that as her cue to walk over to it. She took a seat and rubbed her bloody head wounds. She dialed a few numbers, then looked back at Jackie.

"Is your boss on the way?" Devi asked her.

"Yes, along with the District Attorney. They've agreed to listen to what you have to say."

Devi nodded her head and continued to dial. The call was answered on the first ring.

"Aunt Wanda? I didn't want you to worry where I was. I've been arrested by the Sheriff."

"Everything is in place," Wanda responded.

"I will explain later. Listen to me very carefully. Can you hear me clearly?"

"Yes, Devi, the team is in position."

"I want all my friends to know what happened today. I have been interrogated by the Sheriff for several hours."

"Have they taken the bait?" Wanda chuckled.

"Yes. All of them. Tell them not to worry, but to stay at your house until I contact them."

A deputy entered the room and nodded to Jackie. Jackie looked over at Devi and signaled for her to wrap up the call. Devi continued the charade.

"I'm sorry, Aunt Wanda. I have to go. Just tell everyone not to worry and to stay close."

"My superior, Albert, is here. He wants to talk to you," Jackie said as she eyed Devi with curiosity.

"I didn't even get to call my attorney yet."

"I'll call him for you. Don't worry."

"Ok. Let's deal," Devi said with a note of smugness.

Jackie looked at the deputy before she spoke.

"Cuff her and put her in my SUV. Let Albert know we will meet him there."

"Yes, m'am," the deputy said as he whipped out his handcuffs.

Devi chose not to put up a fight. She held her hands out in front of her and waited to be cuffed. A thought crossed her mind and she pulled her hands away.

"What is it now?" Jackie asked.

"Kolton. He comes with us."

"Ok. Deputy, cuff him and bring him along, too. I'll meet you all downstairs."

By the time they finally reached Shane's house, it was nearly midnight. Devi was tired. So was Kolton. Devi mouthed to him that their ordeal was almost over. That brought him some comfort. He closed his eyes and feigned sleep.

Jackie McKenna and a deputy Devi hadn't seen before, sat in the front seat of Jackie's SUV. Jackie turned to address Devi in the back, but Devi continued to gaze at the house through the windshield of the vehicle.

"Who's house is this?"

"Technically," Devi replied, "it's not mine. All you need to know is what I promised is here."

Jackie hopped out of the car. She briskly walked toward the front of the house. Several deputies carried crow bars and tools as they also exited their vehicles and headed toward the front door of the house. They enter one by one, the way they learned in training. Devi took all this in from her position in the back seat of the SUV. Beads of blood and sweat trickled down her face. Deputies were all over the place now. They frantically screamed things like "Clear!" and "Cover me!"

"Open the garage door!" Jackie bellows.

A deputy opened the garage door and waved Jackie in. She stepped inside. There was a red Mercedes and a black Tesla Roadster parked inside. Devi pressed her face against the SUV back window so she can get a better look. She couldn't help but smirk.

"Get a team in here to move these cares out of the way," Devi heard Jackie order.

A few moments later, Jackie made a beeline for Devi. She opened the door and stared before she spoke.

"I need the keys to the cars."

"I don't have them and I have no idea where they are,' Devi stated truthfully.

Jackie slammed the door shut again. She hesitated before she walked back toward the garage.

"Break the windows out. Put 'em in neutral and push them out of the way. Try not to scratch the paint, though," Jackie barked.

She looked briefly back at Devi. Devi had her face pressed against the window again. Just as the fog began to form on the glass, the window of the Tesla smashed, then the Mercedes. Deputies grunted loudly as they pushed the cars down the driveway.

Devi turned her attention toward the opened front door. A sea of deputies tossed everything about in the house. One agent toyed with an umbrella. He opened it and Devi saw a switch blade pop out.

Devi turned looked toward the garage. Deputies combed every inch of the handyman's quasi workshop that was in a far corner. She lost interest in that quickly and shifted her focus back to the opened front door. She could see a deputy as he attempted to pry open the coat closet. It had been padlocked. Devi had Wanda add that for effect. She snickered at the thought of Wanda when she sneaked over to take care of it.

"What's behind door number ten, ladies and gents?" the deputy bellowed as he finally opened the closet door.

He reached in and grabbed one of many boxes that filled the entire space of the closet. He opened up the box and smiled. He tossed the box to Jackie, who stood with one foot in the house and one foot out as she smoked. She extinguished the cigarette and took the box. She peered inside and realized it was stuffed full of crisp, new cash.

"Ho-ly mo-ly! There's more of these in there?" Jackie asked the deputy.

"Yes, too many to count almost. At least a few hundred. Maybe more."

Jackie sprinted from the house toward Devi.

"Even if no one else believed you, I knew in my gut you were telling the truth."

Devi rolled her eyes.

"I have a question, though."

Devi looked disinterested. Jackie proceeded anyway.

"Who the heck are you?"

"I'm your worst nightmare and your biggest desire, all at once. I'm the thing you hate and the thing you love, all at the same time."

"No. Seriously. Who are you?"

"I am a concerned mother looking out for the best interests of her child. I'm sure you can understand that."

"I can," Jackie said with a tinge of embarrassment in her voice.

"So now that I've returned what Shane was skimming off the top. I would like something returned, too."

"That will have to wait until the Big Guy gets here. Not my call."

"But you don't even know what I want."

"I've gotta wait til-"

Jackie stopped mid-sentence. Clem Dowling pulled up bumper to bumper with Jackie's vehicle. The District Attorney, Jonah Arrington, got out first. Jackie snapped to attention and nodded in the direction of her superiors. Devi did a double take when she saw Clem, Wanda's husband.

"Good morning, sir. We've recovered several hundred boxes filled with cash and product, thanks to good detective work and this woman," Jackie says as she pointed toward Devi.

Clem eyed Devi, but he didn't recognize her. It was a whole other lifetime ago the last time he saw her. She was a child then and he still had morals and integrity, as much as a meth addict could have, anyway.

"I'd like something in return for my help, Uncle Clem."

Surprise filled the air and everyone snapped their neck toward Devi. Clem's eyes narrowed to slits. He couldn't place her.

"I want the women you stole released. All of them," Devi continued.

"Women we stole?" Jackie asked incredulously.

"Yes. They told me all about your little human trafficking operation."

Jackie smirks and Clem laughs from deep within his belly.

"I see someone's been doing some homework. What do you care what we do with a few drug whores? Their lives aren't worth a plug nickel, at least not til we sell 'em and give 'em some kind of purpose in this life," Clem explained.

"Says the king of the drug whores," Devi said as she rolled her eyes.

"You'd better watch your mouth, Princes!" Jackie said as she charged toward Devi, night stick out.

Clem put his arm out to halt Jackie.

"Let her talk, Jackie."

"I want the women released and the children. I also want my cousin's body released to her mother. Allison. And then I want to get as far away as possible and forget this town even exists."

"What are you talking about? Allison, who?"

"Your daughter. Allison. Her mother can't even grieve properly because you won't release the body. Calling her "evidence," Devi said as she glared at Jackie.

She continued, "And on top of it all, you had the unmitigated gall to kidnap her baby. I want him, too."

Clem looked around the front yard. His fury was evident. He made eye contact with Rennick, who just exited the house.

"You fool! You killed my daughter?"

Before Rennick can answer, BLAM! Jonah Arrington shot him just above his nose. Rennick landed with a thud in the grass and died with his eyes wide open.

Clem muttered incoherently. Then he turned to Jackie and orders "Let them all go! How many did we take in?"

"Take in? Like you're running a bed and breakfast?" Devi asked sarcastically.

"I just wanted to make something of myself," Clem spun around and said to Devi. "I spent so many years as a worthless junkie myself."

He paused and turned his attention toward the Sheriff before he continued.

"I said, how many did we take in last week, Jackie!"

"Five women, sir and nine children," Jackie stated matter of factly.

"Release all of them. Devi here brought my money and my product back home. It's the least we can do to say thank you."

"But I want them brough to my Aunt Wanda's house. That way they'll have a place to clean up before they go home."

"Consider it done," Clem said.

"And one more thing. I want Jackie to take me to meet them."

"I am not-"

"Done! She returned product that you let slip away. You'll take her!" Clem interrupted.

"Yes, sir," Jackie managed to reply.

"How did that incompetent idiot kill my daughter?"

"Buprenorphine. Just like the others."

Clem wept.

"Uncle Clem-"

"Why do you insist on calling me that?"

"Rhonda's daughter. Devi. You don't recognize me? Seriously?"

Clem studied Devi's face.

"Drugs have literally fried my brain and many of my best memories, girl. Lined my pockets, but ruined my brain and my life."

"Let's go." Jackie said to Devi as she snapped her fingers.

"Someone is bringing the women ad children?" Devi wanted to know.

"Yes, Princess, yes."

"Please release my cousin's body to Morgan Funeral Home. I can take it from there. Where is her baby?" Devi said as she looked at Clem.

"He'll be returned."

Devi inhaled deeply, held it, then exhaled. A weight had been lifted. Jackie hopped into her SUV and started the engine. Devi slid into the front passenger seat. As they backed out of the driveway, Devi snuck a peek at Kolton. He looked to be peacefully asleep in the back seat, but he gave Devi a peace sign and a smile.

When they arrived at Wanda's, Wanda greeted Devi and Kolton with a huge hug. She greeted Jackie with a frown and unhidden disdain. Twenty four loggers filled the living room, ready to pounce on Jackie should she make any sudden moves. Ralph Wyant, one of the loggers, had already called Devi's contact at the FBI. They were on their way to get Jackie.

"The baby will be back soon," Devi shared with Wanda.

Wanda wept. Devi studied her for a moment before she spoke again.

"The women are coming, too. They can all clean up and finally have a good night's rest before they face the world again."

"But we can go home now, right, Mom?" Kolton asked.

"Yes, sir! We can definitely go home now!" Devi said, joy finally in her heart again.

The doorbell rang. The women and children had arrived. Once the last woman enters the house, the loggers pounce the deputy who has brought them, as well as Jackie. They tie the pair up and let them know that their just desserts will be served on a silver platter soon.

"Ladies, make yourself at home. You are safe. We will figure out a plan for you going forward. But tonight, you can rest in peace here."

One woman was already asleep on the sofa, wrapped in a blanket. Devi approached her. She tapped her on the shoulder. The woman jumped like a scared cat. Bead of sweat flowed from her brow and she shook uncontrollably.

"Hun, come on into one of the bedrooms and lie down. You're safe now."

Their eyes met.

"Allison? Allison!"

Allison is disoriented and in a fog, but she smiled.

"Devi? Is that you?"

"Yes, it's me. Wanda! Get over here!"

Devi embraced Allison. Wanda walks up and can't believe her eyes.

"Is it you, baby girl?"

Wanda ugly sobs. Allison reaches out to hug her, but stumbles. Wanda catches her and they embrace.

"All I kept thinking about, Mama, was you and little Randall. I knew if I could just hold on to the two of you, I'd be fine."

Wanda cries louder. The doorbell rings. Devi answers it. An FBI agent has brought the children.

"I'm not sure if the mothers are all here, but let's reunite who we can. And I have a few other agents with me to take care of your VIPs. I assume that's them over there," the agent says as he points to Jackie and the deputy, tied up at the dining room table..

"And that other situation has been taken care of? With the District Attorney and his people?" Devi asked

"Yes it has. Thanks for the tips. We've been trying to put the pieces of this case together for more than two years. We owe you."

"I still haven't put all the pieces together myself. Just the ones that matter most, I suppose," Devi said with relief.

"Great work, Devi."

The agent turned to leave, but then jerked to a halt and turned around to speak again.

"I almost forgot. There is an infant whom I am supposed to put directly in your arms."

Devi smiles. Wanda and Allison grin from ear to ear and cry.

The agent jogged to his vehicle and returned with Baby Randall. Devi kissed his forehead gently as the agent waved goodbye. Devi admired the sleeping baby and rocked him as she walked toward his mother and grandmother.

"Your mommy's home, Randall," Devi said, as Wanda squealed with joy. Allison was speechless, with tears in her eyes as she took her baby and held him close. They were finally home and they were never leaving again, she thought.

Devi and Kolton didn't hang around for long. There were ready to get back to their own home, far, far away. After they told everyone goodbye, they nearly sprinted to Devi's truck and sped away. Kolton scanned the radio and stopped on a song he liked. He took in all of the early morning scenery. It was just past sunrise.

"Who knew such beauty could harbor such evil?" Kolton said to Devi.

"No kidding!"

"Did you tell them it was Clem who was behind it all?"

"I left that for the FBI to do," Devi chuckled.

"I would have, too!" Kolton exclaimed.

They both laughed heartily. They were interrupted by the ringing of Devi's phone. They both eyeball it. Kolton picked it up from the seat between them and looked at the caller ID.

"It's the magazine. I bet they want you to research another story."

Devi rolled her window down. Kolton leaned over and pitched the phone through it and out onto the freeway. They both laughed raucously and Devi picked up the pace.

Michelle enjoys hearing from readers. You can contact her/give her feedback by emailing her at info@kmpentertainment.org

You can keep up with her projects by going to her company's website www.kmpentertainment.org or via Facebook at the KMP Entertainment page, https://www.facebook.com/KMPEntertainment/

The next adventure that awaits you is titled TWO JUNKIES AND A DEMON. Find out what happens when the depravity of a sprawling city's drug culture, violence, and a brazen liar intersects with grace, mercy and love. Available soon! Watch the KMP Entertainment Facebook page and website for updates.